The Heart's Dark Hunger: Part One
White Buffalo MCs Book 2
Dark Horse's Story

By
Trinity Blacio

The Heart's Dark Hunger
Copyright 2018 by Trinity Blacio
ISBN: 978-1-68361-315-2
Cover art by Fantasia Frog

Published by Decadent Publishing Company, LLC
Look for us online at:
www.decadentpublishing.com

The Heart's Dark Hunger

Dark Horse, the enforcer, for the White Buffalo MC is as dark as they come. Nothing or no one will stand in his way from collecting what is his, Lilly.

Her smile, her soul is the light he needs in his life. The light that died so long ago when his mother was murdered. Now someone else threatens to take what is his, but he is old enough to fight. The enemy had better run, because he won't stop until they are dead.

Lilly has a small gift, but she thought nothing would hurt her, and she was wrong. She didn't listen in the past, but as her world collapses around her, can she push past the fear to stand beside the Dark Warrior who has come to claim her? He controls her body, but can Lilly allow him to capture her heart?
This warrior isn't leaving her side anytime soon.

Also by Trinity Blacio

Hunger of the Heart

Warriors of old used to ride their mighty horses out into the night, searching for the enemy, hunting for food, and enjoying the land the Great Mother let them borrow. Those times have changed, and greedy men have taken their land. Cities, roads fill their once-quiet world.

Born on separate reservations, a group of young men with hearts of old souls, long dead warrior's' souls, ride together again, but this time they don't ride horses. Today, it's all about the motorcycle. Helping the desperate, following the call of the ancient spirits.

They call themselves The White Buffalo MC, and it's their job to get their people ready for the dark day, which was told to them long ago.

Chapter One

*"One more night dreaming of my White Lilly. Your silky skin
will crave my dark loving, like the lilies crave the water and sun."*
Dark Horse, Enforcer of the White Buffalo MC

"It's going to take us close to eleven hours to get to
Douglassville, and that is without breaks. I want a layout of the area,
businesses and anything that will give us an idea what we are up
against when we hit this town. The Irons know we are coming; they
will have full advantage over us." Running Wolf glanced at his wife,
next to him, again.

Yep, his friend was a goner. Dark Horse sat back, watching his
best friend and the protectiveness he showed toward his wife, but
then again, he'd be no different, if not worse.

"The town really isn't a town. It's got about three hundred
people living there, well, did have until the Irons settled in. We have
no idea how many now. Do you know how many members in the
Irons group?" she questioned.

Running Wolf leaned over and placed a kiss on her cheek.
"Don't worry so much, Little Gypsy, we'll get there in time." His
friend's gaze met his. "They call her Lilly, but we don't know if that
is her actual name. I've had Night Wind trying to get a list of people
there and their homes. So far, no Lilly's. But, Gypsy hasn't seen the
pictures of the homes. It's one of the reasons she is sitting in on this
meeting." Running Wolf took a drink of his coffee as Kizzy snorted.

"Like you could stop me from coming. Here, burp your

daughter so I can see if I recognize anything." She placed a cloth diaper over Running Wolf's shoulder before handing their daughter to him.

Kizzy turned her gaze on him. "If we can find out where she lives, you guys can do your thing on your bikes, and my uncles and I can run in there and grab her before they even know what is going on. She will be scared of any man at first, so having me there to talk to her will help."

"No!" Running Wolf snapped.

She rolled her eyes and patted his arm. "Relax. You know my uncles are just as protective as you are. They won't allow me anywhere near the place if there is danger, but I need to be there or she won't go to you guys. She'll just see another biker group. You know I'm right."

"I have to agree with Running Wolf on this, little sister. Your life is just as important as hers. You can talk to her after everything is settled. I don't want you in the middle of anything. If you were mine, you would be heading to Canada, but I know you are needed, and I appreciate everything you and Running Wolf are doing," Dark Horse told her.

Kizzy waved her hand at him. "It's nothing. Now, let's see these pictures."

For the next few minutes, Dark Horse watched her flip through the air photos Night Wind had gotten until she stopped at one picture and lifted it up. She lifted the next one and put it next to the one she was holding. "This is it. This is where she stays. I don't know if it's her home, but it's the one I've seen in my dreams." She handed them to Dark Horse, and he nodded.

"Yes, I recognize the building in the back." He held up his hand, stopping Kizzy from saying anything. "I've had a few dreams about her, too." His gaze went to Running Wolf. "We don't have long. I don't think she'll last."

"She'll last. She is as strong as you are." Soaring Eagle came up behind him and set his hand on his shoulder. "Our problem is going to be the traps that lie waiting for us and getting there. The Great Mother has claimed another small town this morning. Knoxville, Tennessee, as we know it, is gone.

"What happened?" Dark Horse sat up straight as their old friend and mentor took a seat next to him.

Soaring sighed. "Greed and fracking is what happened. The poisoned water used for this drilling ran into the city's drinking water so that no one could drink it. Sort of like the town in West Virginia. The city is there, but they are cut off right now from what I've heard."

Dark Horse nodded. "I've heard that, too. "It's all over the news. I never did like the idea of fracking, was always against it, but so many people are so desperate, just like we were." He turned his attention toward Running Wolf who nodded.

"I was wrong, and I can only hope the Great Mother can forgive me for that. I didn't sign the contracts when Lone Star brought them to me. I just couldn't do it." Running Wolf patted his daughter's back, at which she released a solid burp.

"She knows you were only trying to help your people," Soaring Eagle reassured Running Wolf but turned his gaze on Dark Horse. "This trip is going to be a hard one on you. You've never settled down after your mother passed. But I truly believe with this Lilly standing next to you, there will be nothing to stop you from achieving your goals. Now, we should get going. My horse is loaded in the trailer, and we are ready." The old man stood and moved toward the door.

"That man impresses me each and every day. I swear. Where does he get the strength?" Kizzy stood and stretched. "Give me our little one. I'll strap her in the car seat while you get everyone moving."

Running Wolf nodded to him as Dark Horse followed his best friend's wife outside to their car. Nothing would get by him. His sister gypsy would always be protected as long as he was around. He shifted his body to place it in front of Kizzy as she strapped their little one in the car seat only to see Jay Bird coming toward him.

"Do you need help with something?" he questioned scanning around them.

"Soaring Eagle sent me over here. It seems our paths are going the same way. Not only will you meet your Lilly, but Soaring Eagle believes my forever woman will be in Texas also. I would like to be your right-hand man when we arrive, your enforcer, if it is all right with you.

Dark Horse had worked with Jay Bird before and knew he was as deadly as they came, great with all sorts of weapons. And his appearance was totally deceiving—Jay Bird always smiled and projected calmness to others, yet the man waited to strike like a cobra. "I would be honored to have you at my side." He held out his hand, shaking it. "We worked well together, last time. Are you going to call your family in?"

Kizzy closed the door behind him and stepped up to his side.

He glanced down at her. "You all set?"

"Yep, just waiting for Running Wolf, and here he comes."

Running Wolf nodded to Jay Bird then pulled his woman into

his arms.

"I've talked with Soaring Eagle. We have about twenty men who will be staying with you and Jay Bird in Texas. Plus, those 45 who will meet us there. You'll have enough to protect yourselves once we leave. I've also instructed the men to have their families start packing up and meet us there next week. That will give us the time to get rid of this threat and clean things up."

"Excellent. I just informed Jay Bird to call his family also," Dark Horse said.

"The only one I have is my little sister and my uncle's family. They will be following us to Texas. We'll speak again at our next stop," Jay Bird nodded to him and Running Wolf then spun around and moved to his bike.

"That was a pleasant man." Kizzy got into the passenger seat.

Running Wolf snorted. "He might appear like it, Little Gypsy, but I've seen him skin a man who was raping a little girl. He is just as deadly as Dark Horse. Never forget, each of my men have a specialty."

Dark Horse smiled when Kizzy shivered. "What is your specialty?"

"You don't want to know, little sister, but it will be used always to protect your family. Be careful driving. Things are getting dicey now." Dark Horse moved toward his new-age horse, Flames. He smiled, running his hand over his 1970 Harley Sportster, his baby. One day soon, his Lilly would be riding behind him, holding onto him. "We're coming, my Lilly, hold on," He swung his leg over his bike then started it. It was time for his journey to begin.

*****

The dust was thick as the leather belt that had been used on her two nights ago by Fuzz, the leader of the Irons. The left side of her face was swollen so bad, she couldn't see out of her left eye. But she was lucky. Her father had been allowed to go away in an ambulance. His heart wasn't strong, but if he made it, he was free of the Irons, and that was all that mattered. Sometimes being a nurse was a good thing and other times not so good.

She reached up and shut the blinds on her front windows, hoping most of the sand would stay outside, but it was a losing battle with two of her windows busted from Fat Bob's rage the last time they had driven out here. The same time Fuzz had taken his anger out on her because she dared to call the ambulance for her father. Yes, she had taken a beating, but he hadn't killed her. She was here to serve a purpose, he had told the group of thugs he rode with.

"Fucking gift," she growled and rubbed her arms. If they hadn't heard about her gift in the damn hospital she'd be okay, but no, the blabbermouth drunk in town just couldn't shut the hell up. Now, Fuzz owned her, at least that is what he claimed. But Lilly knew something he didn't. The man would die. A shiver went down her spine as she remembered the way he would die, stretched out in the dirt, tied to four wooden posts.

She sighed, closing her eyes for just a second, picturing the man that was coming, the one who would end Fuzz's life.

Her white knight, or Dark Horse, he called himself. His dark hair braided with a single eagle feather in the back. Lilly moaned as her nipples grew hard and the inside of her legs grew damp.

"I can't do this," she whispered, shaking herself out of the daydream and once more checking all the locks on the doors and windows. Yes, Dark Horse would be the man who would truly own her body and soul, if she had enough courage.

Lilly shut and locked the back door, before heading up the back stairs.

"Dark Horse," she called out to him as if he would hear her. Would he reach Texas in time? Lilly didn't know how much longer she could survive. She had been lucky this time and hadn't needed to go to the hospital, because there was no way they would have allowed her to leave. Hell, would Dark Horse and his friends survive? Already, the Irons were preparing for them. She hadn't told them that the White Buffalos were coming. No, someone else had and so far, their attempts to warn them away wasn't stopping them.

Turning around on the bottom step, Lilly stared at what was left of her once-beautiful home. Windows broken, furniture destroyed, and many pictures ripped up in hopes she would join their little biker group. She had been born in this house, her mother dying in the room upstairs at the age of fifty from cancer.

The last time they had partied outside, her front and back yards had been destroyed. It had taken her a whole day to clean up their disgusting mess they had left.

The men didn't give a shit about any female, fucking them anytime they wanted and anywhere. She moved slowly up the stairs, hoping tonight would be a quiet one. That the beating he had given her would be enough to keep him away for a few days. It had been before, but he was crazy enough to change his mind.

Turning on the light in the bathroom, Lilly stared in the mirror above the sink and winced. It was three times worse than yesterday, but, as a nurse, she knew it would get worse before it got better.

She proceeded to brush out the dried blood before getting in the shower. She wanted to soak in the tub, but god knew if they would show up again. Tears filled her eyes at the pain. She had given herself four stitches on her head where the belt buckle had sliced into her, shaving the one spot that appeared to be the worse of her wounds, but she'd be damn if she'd chop off all of her hair.

New clothes, Lilly put the brush down and moved into her bedroom, a room she now couldn't stand to be in. The place where he had taken her, over and over again. She grabbed her sweat pants and T-shirt, the ugliest clothes she owned, taking a quick peek outside through her window but seeing no one. "Please not tonight," she whispered and moved back to the bathroom, needing to scrub herself clean.

Tonight, she would sleep in her parents' room, as she had been for the past three nights, ever since the last night he had raped her. Placing her clothes on the counter, she stepped into the tub and turned on the shower. The water was hot, making her skin pink just like she loved, but Lilly didn't linger, grabbing the soap and scrubbing, trying to get his scent off her skin and maybe even out of her memory, but she knew that wouldn't work. Careful of her stitches, Lilly quickly washed her hair before shutting off the water.

Five minutes, a new record for her. Lilly wrapped her hair in the towel and put her sweats on before returning to the kitchen and grabbing a can of soda out of the fridge. She'd have to go to the store tomorrow, and Lilly dreaded it. It would give Fuzz a reason to visit her, but unless she wanted to starve, there was no way around it.

Lilly moved up to her parents' room and climbed on their bed, staring out the window as she started the process of brushing out her hair.

Taking a sip of her pop and pulling the towel from her head, Lilly froze. The bed shook. Hell, the whole house shook, and the lights flickered. Lilly watched in horror as a deep ravine opened up outside and all the power went out. Trees fell all around till the shaking stopped. Putting her pop on the stand, Lilly wiped her hand off where it had spilled and moved downstairs, needing to see what had happened.

Dust filled the air as she stepped out onto the porch. When the air cleared, Lilly couldn't believe what she was seeing. The hole that opened up had to be at least twelve feet wide. Lilly circled around her house, shaking her head. Her house was sitting in the middle of nowhere now. She had about fifteen feet from her house to the drop off. It was the weirdest thing she had ever seen. Her house was cut off from everything...

She smiled almost relieved. They wouldn't be able to get to her. Then Lilly heard the bikes. Her heart beat fast. Lilly swore she tasted fear and it made her sick to her stomach.

She ran inside, slamming the door behind her, and curled up on the floor, peeking out the corner window. "Well he sure couldn't blame me for this one, but it's sure going to piss him off," Lilly mumbled, seeing the first bike ride up to where the road dropped. Fat Bob frowned, studying the ravine before he turned his attention toward the house.

Lilly shivered and ran upstairs to get a better view, knowing that if Fat Bob was around, Fuzz would be coming anytime soon.

Sure enough, Fuzz rolled up next to Fat Bob and got off his bike. He paced back and forth yelling, but what had her laughing was when both Fat Bob and Fuzz stumbled backward as a big piece of land on the other side broke away, taking their bikes with it.

Never had Lilly felt such satisfaction as she did watching the two men glaring at the hole below as more of their group showed up behind them. Fuzz glanced from the hole to her house glaring daggers, sending a shiver down her spine. The man was not done with her by a long shot.

Fuzz climbed on the back of one of his men's bikes as did Fat Bob, and they rode back toward the town.

With the sun setting, Lilly hurried around the house, pulling out candles and such, knowing she wasn't going to get power anytime soon. Her dad had installed a generator in the basement, but Lilly wasn't even going to bother with that since there was nothing in the fridge that would spoil and the freezer was empty. All she had were the dry goods and military rations her father had kept for emergency. She would have to check out his stash in the basement later'.

But for now, Lilly lit a few candles in the bedroom, and proceeded to comb out her hair, braiding it. Tonight, she would be able to sleep, Lilly was safe for now.

Lilly took a sip of her pop and had crawled under the covers when her cell phone rang.

"I swear, as soon as I get settled," she grumbled and ran to her room for her phone. The sheriff's number popped up on the display. "Fuck."

She answered. "What do you want Craig?"

"I thought you would want an update on your dad. He's doing okay and has stabilized. How are you doing? I heard you are kind of stranded there?"

"Really? Do you think I'm stupid? I know Fuzz is there with you. It's pretty sad when our local police have to join a biker gang while the people who voted for you are suffering. Fuck off, Craig, and don't call me again," she snapped, shutting the phone off before he could say another word.

It might not have been a smart thing to do, but that man gave her the creeps. Plus, he had been there when Fuzz had raped her and done nothing but watched.

Closing her eyes, Lilly took a deep breath, trying to calm herself. Craig only called when he wanted information or to hassle her. To think she used to date the asshole, before all hell broke loose around her small town, six months ago. Six months, and nothing was the same, her town, her body, her home. With that depressing thought, Lilly moved back to her bed, crawling in and covering herself after blowing out the candles.

"No nightmares please," she whispered, hoping for dreams of her dark knight or horse.

Chapter Two

*My White Lilly might have lived in fear, and tears, but soon
she will have the love her soul seeks, but is afraid to reach for."*
Dark Horse, Enforcer of the White Buffalo MC

Dark Horse sat on his metal horse watching his surroundings as
Running Wolf and Kizzy, ran into the diner to get some food, and do
a pit stop, stretching their legs. He munched on a Whopper he had
picked up earlier. They had decided to stop in Nashville, before
heading out again. People moved around town like there was
nothing to worry about.

Oh, he had heard on the news broadcast about a few incidents,
but so far no one was putting the signs together. He tilted his head
to the side, staring at the window across the way. Popping the last
bite of sandwich in his mouth, he slid off this bike and nodded to
Sun Bull. "I'm going to run across the street."

"Go. We got this." His friend stuffed a fry into his mouth.

Dark Horse snorted and made his way across the street. In the
window of an antique store, an old wooden box called to him, and
Dark Horse never ignored the voice inside him.

Inside the shop, an elderly lady lifted her head and smiled at
him from behind the counter. "Can I help you with something?"

"The box in the window, with the lily on it, would you mind if I
take a look at it?" He smiled at the woman.

"Of course." She came around the counter. "It's really one of a
kind. My husband found it about forty years ago in an old barn he

13

was working on." The small woman reached in the window and drew the box out. Turning to him, she opened it. "We found out these old carvings tell a story about the flower. They called this the hope box."

"My late mother used to tell me this story when I was a boy," he explained, not knowing why he gave her this information. He gently took the antique. "I'll buy it. Know this will go to a great woman. She needs a new beginning."

The woman returned to the counter. "I know it will. I have one more thing you might like. Follow me."

Dark Horse was twice her size and he knew his appearance was sometimes intimidating to others, but not to this little lady. But what he wasn't expecting was for her to pull out an old hunting knife.

"I usually have a great eye when it to comes to people. When I found this last year in one of the auctions, I had to have it. Something kept telling me to purchase it and now I know why. It was meant to be yours."

The knife had an ivory handle, a copper blade over eight inches long and the ridges in it would kill anything as it was pulled out. An inscription scrolled along the side. May the Great Mother take you back into her open arms. Yes, this one knife had been made by one of his people. He picked it up, amazed at how well it fit into his hand.

"The woman is right. That was meant for you, both the box and the knife," Soaring Eagle informed him, scaring the living crap out of him.

"Old man, don't do that," Dark Horse grumbled, earning a snort from the medicine man. "Only you and Running Wolf can do that to me."

"You were really into that knife." Kizzy stepped up next to him.

"I knew you were here, little sister. How could anyone not? You jingle when you walk, plus the little mite there was cooing too loud." Dark Horse leaned down and placed a kiss on the top of her daughter's head.

"Well, we didn't want you throwing that thing at us, now, did we?" Kizzy countered.

"You, my dear, are a menace." He returned his attention to the woman behind the counter. "I'll take them both. How much do I owe you?"

"Nothing for the knife. You were meant to have that, but for the lily box, sixty should be fine," the old woman informed him.

"That is for both." He handed her a hundred-dollar bill. "Tough times are coming. Please take care."

The woman smiled and took his money. "I won't be long for this world. My husband has left already and is waiting for me. I've done my living. Now it's up to you young folk to carry on for us. Remember our world as it was."

"That we will do." Kizzy pointed to a book up on one of the shelves high up. "Can you reach that for me?"

"Where is your husband?" he grumbled and moved over to her, hearing the door to the little shop open.

"Right here. She had me run to the other store to pick up snacks for later. Knew you were in here or she wouldn't be in here by herself," Running Wolf grumbled.

Dark Horse took the big book down and was going to hand it to her, but there was no way she was going to be able to hold it with the baby in her arms.

He set the book down and reached for their little girl. "Come here, beauty." He took the bundle of cuteness into his arms and placed a kiss on the little girl's forehead. "Now, you can browse while I get my baby fill."

Kizzy smiled and stepped up, placing a kiss on his cheek before Running Wolf could stop her. "You are an amazing man, and your Lilly is very lucky to have you." She patted his shoulder as his friend wrapped his arm around her.

"Stop kissing my men." He nipped her neck as she giggled, opening the book.

"That is one of the oldest history books that I know of. It was written in 1902 but bound at a later date. Hi, my name is Lilly." The older woman Said.

"I should have known. The name fits you, and it has been a pleasure to do business with you." Dark Horse reached over and took her hand, placing a kiss on her knuckles.

The older woman blushed and pulled her hand away. "Thank you, kind sir. You have made this old lady's day."

"My lady, you are not old. The light dancing in your eyes is still bright." He stated the truth.

The woman rolled her eyes at him. "You are a smooth one. Your Lilly will have a good life with you young man. Anyone can say pretty words, but with you, a person can see they come from the heart."

Dark Horse buried his face into tiny Miranda's neck.

. "I do believe you have embarrassed our warrior," Kizzy reached over and squeezed his arm, laughing then turned her attention to the shop lady. "I would like this book. Do you have any others books like it? I'm trying to build a small library, so any help would be appreciated?"

Running Wolf took his daughter from him. "One more night and we'll be there, but already I'm hearing from our scouts they have found traps. Tonight, we'll plan our route. Kizzy's uncle is going to drive the car in after the area is secure."

Dark Horse frowned. "And you will be?"

"I'll be riding right beside you when we enter that town."

"No, you cannot." Dark Horse nodded to Kizzy who was sorting through books. "You, my friend, have too much to live for. I will not have you risk your life helping me."

"And you have a say in this?" Running Wolf challenged.

"Damn it, Running Wolf, how am I going to concentrate on what is ahead of us if I have you next to me," Dark Horse snapped.

"There is no need to worry. You two will live through this fight," Soaring Eagle said. "He is to ride beside you once more before you two go your separate ways till this thing is over."

"Do you see how many will survive?" Dark Horse asked.

Soaring Eagle shook his head. "I'm afraid the Great Mother wouldn't even know this. With all the panic that will go on, well people do stupid things when scared we all know this."

Dark Horse sighed. "Any more towns go down?"

"A few overseas. So far nothing around here, but that could change any time. The way the people are polluting the ground and air." Soaring Eagle shook his head. "I thought I would never see this day, but we as a species we have gotten too greedy, always searching for ways to make our lives easier. Taking and taking and not giving back. It was bound to happen."

"Every species panics when things change." Kizzy pointed to the stack of books on the counter. "How about I take the baby and you grab those?"

Running Wolf couldn't help but laugh. "I have a feeling by the time you two get to Canada, you will have that library she wants, among other things."

"Don't be laughing. I've been picking up things for your woman and your place. You'll need stuff, too, and right now your Lilly is just surviving. We need to help you."

Dark Horse bowed his head. "Once more, you have surprised me. I should have been thinking of this also."

"Dark Horse, you're worried about Lilly, and you should be. You let me do this while you two figure out how to get rid of those other bikers without killing anyone around her town."

"We'll do our best." Running Wolf handed Miranda to Kizzy and kissed her cheek. "Come on. You get to help carry some this stuff out to the trailer. Bring your box, too. We'll keep it in the trailer till we get there."

Dark Horse slid the knife into its sheath, drawing Running Wolf's attention. "Can I see it?"

He handed the ivory-handled knife to his friend who whistled. "Haven't seen this kind of workmanship in a while. Yep, this one is yours, my friend. Even I can see that." He handed it back to him, paid for the books then gave the store owner a little extra.

She started to argue with Running Wolf, but he insisted. "Keep it. Close up early and do something you haven't done in a while. Treat yourself." Running Wolf grabbed a stack of books as did Dark Horse, balancing the box on top of them with the knife tucked in his back pocket for now.

Two more days, and he would have his lady beside him. From that day forth, she wouldn't leave his sight.

***

Lilly shot out of bed, grabbing at the covers, and scanned her surroundings. Nothing, no Fuzz or any other. She climbed out of bed and peered out the window

The new ravine was still there, but what she saw on the other side had her shaking. It would seem the whole damn biker team was had assembled.

'And the idiots were trying to throw a rope across the way. "Please don't let this happen," she whispered. So far, they weren't succeeding.

The men parted and Lilly saw Fat Bob on one of the bikes. He was going to try and jump the ravine. "My god, not him, please." Her stomach knotted, and her hands started to shake. She had to block all her doors because if Fat Bob got in her house she'd die under his hands. Halfway down the stairs, she heard the screams. She flew to the downstairs window just in time to see Fat Bob and the bike sink into the ground. His screams mixed with those of the other bikers who jumped on their bikes and roared away.

Lilly released the breath she'd holding. She'd never wished anyone bodily harm, but these men cared about nothing or no one.

At the bend in the road, one bike stopped, and the rider turned to stare at the house. That expression and it was one of death, hers or his, Lilly didn't know. Then she smelled the fire and glanced behind her to see smoke rolling down the stairs. With a whimper, Lilly grabbed the quilt off the sofa, matches and some candles, and dashed toward the back of the house, going for the underground bunker her father had built a long time ago, hoping it would be safe enough. It was her only chance at surviving this mess.

Out on the back porch, Lilly glanced around but saw no one as she pushed aside the hidden door on the porch floor to reveal the metal door to the bunker.

She let the door clang closed behind her and stopped, allowing her eyes to adjust to the darkness, as she dropped the blanket and one candle to light the other. As soon as she did, Lilly carefully inched down the rest of the stairs. She'd come back for the other stuff as soon as she knew what was down there.

But Lilly should have known her father would have been ready. As soon as she stepped onto the cement flooring, fluorescent lights flickered as they came on, surprising her totally.

All around her were supplies, a bed, even a composting toilet off to the back in a separate little room.

"Papa," she whispered, tears filling her eyes. Lilly set her candle down and blew it out before she exploring the main room. It was twice the size of their bottom floor of her house, but what caught her eye was the note on a control panel.

My Dear Princess,

Her hand shook, and tears filled her eyes as she sat down on the sofa, he had placed down here. Her father, was he still alive? A single tear dripped on the paper.

As you know of my gift, I knew this day would come. I have tried to prepare this area for you without drawing the attention of our so-called sheriff. Do not trust him, my Lilly.

Lilly snorted at those words, knowing how true they were.

I just wish I could have saved you from their dirty hands. That is my failure, but in my heart, I see your man coming. This safe place will keep you from harm's way till he comes. There is enough food for two weeks. I know you don't like those kind of toilets, but you'll have to learn to use them, princess. Your food supplies are in the other room. The electricity is solar powered by panels a distance from the house. Just know, you'll have power for as long as you are down there. If you click on the top lever to the right, the cameras will come on. Being an electrician did come in handy. I have set up cameras in a few places through town and around our home so you'll know what is coming.

"Daddy," she whispered, flicking on the switch. Above her, on the walls, monitors came to life, ten of them. One showed the road coming into town, another downtown itself, two on the road toward her house, and others showing her property, which started more tears rolling down her face. Her home was in total flames, now. There would soon be nothing left. Pictures, clothes everything burned above her. "Everything gone," she whispered, taking a deep breath.

Put the letter down and open the red door.

Lilly frowned but did as her father ordered.

Another light came on, and she blinked, standing there staring at things she recognized from the house. "How?" she spoke out loud in awe at all the things she had believed had been destroyed.

"My laptop," she squealed, stepping in and grabbing it, hugging it to her. Then saw the photo albums, her mother's possessions, and her father's. Everything that had been important to them was in this treasure trove. "Thank you, Daddy," she whispered, moving back to the sofa and placing the laptop next to her.

I couldn't tell you what I was doing and risk those monsters would find this place. I knew you would need it in the end. I don't know if I'll see you again, but know I love you, and I'm very proud of you.

Daddy

Lilly sat there and just cried, holding the letter to her heart while staring at the monitors. Finally, needing something to drink, Lilly went searching in the pantry room, laughing, seeing all the diet pop she loved, next to stacks and stacks of bottled water. Yes, her father had thought of everything. Grabbing a bottle of water, Lilly glanced to the left, smiling. "God, I love you, Daddy." She grabbed the new coffee pot and one of the bags of ground coffee and it back into the main room to search for a plug.

Sure enough, her father had eight plugs, in one area, with a note.

Watch your usage you don't want to use up the charge. During the day, the solar input will recharge everything, but at night, use candles if you can.

She read further how to turn off the lights and other things. She would even be able to go online via a satellite Internet connection.

"So smart, Daddy." She went about making her coffee then noticed the Irons driving into her small town, parking their bikes in front of the little police station. "You mother fucker." The sheriff came out of his office with one of the bimbos from the Irons attached to his side.

Lilly sat at the little table near the plugs and turned her computer on to research these White Buffalo men that Fuzz kept asking about. She needed to know everything about them before she could trust them. Even though the man in her dreams had her body humming with sexual awareness, she wasn't about to allow her heart to get hurt. She had protected it so far and wasn't about to turn it over to just any hot man.

It took her a while, and a cup of strong coffee, but she was connected to the Internet and on the White Buffalo's' main web page. From what she could see, there was nothing but good reviews and stories of this group.

Lilly sucked in her breath when a picture of three men, the president, Running Wolf, another named Sun Bull, and the man of her dreams, Dark Horse, popped up. She took a sip of coffee, staring at the man in question. There was no doubt in her mind that this man was going to be part of her life, but could she give him her heart? Could he be what she craved? A man strong enough to take total control over her heart and body. Lilly knew she was different. All throughout high school dating she hadn't been able to find that one man. But staring at this picture, she only hoped he was the one.

Lilly found an email and wondered if it would work. They might as well know there were traps all around her town, if they were really coming her way. Lilly worked on explaining why she was contacting them, hoping she didn't sound like some nut case. She read the letter over three times before sending it off, hoping someone important would open it in time.

She peeked over at the small toilet and sighed. "All right, Daddy. I'm trying the stupid thing." It wasn't too bad, but the idea of cleaning it out did not sit well with her. At least she wouldn't be able to smell it. She used the hand sanitizer before going to get one of the MRE's. She had tried them out before, and they hadn't been half bad. But weeks of them might be a problem.

Her computer dinged as she sat back down, opening up her meal.

Dear Lilly,

I can't thank you enough for your warning. My name is Kizzy, and I'm married to Running Wolf. We should be there soon. We are well aware of the traps these ass-wipes have set for our men. Oh, by the way, on phone so this is slow going here. When we stop again, I'll have Dark Horse personally write you. Are you safe for now?

Why would she inform Dark Horse? Did they know something? Lilly tore open her food then checked the monitors again. The Irons were still all around the sheriff's, but what had her worried was the sheriff staring down at his phone. "Fuck." She opened up a new email account, one she knew the ass wouldn't be able to track, and wrote back to Kizzy.

Kizzy,

I'm sorry to say, but I believe our local police has access to my old email. Please, be careful.

Lilly.

She got up and paced, watching the monitors. Three of the bikers were now coming her way. "Please don't be able to see the hidden door," she whispered, scanning her house and the surrounding area.

She could see nothing but burned ruins. Even via the one camera trained on where the back door used to be, Lilly could see nothing. Three men stood by the ravine, staring at the burned-out mess. One walked to the right, the others other to the left. Lilly knew they were trying to see the back yard, but she knew they'd see nothing since her door was now buried in a flaming mess.

Lilly crawled up the stairs and placed her hand on the door but yanked it back just as quickly. The door was hot, but not enough to melt it. So, she was safe for the time being. "Sure, would be nice if it rained." She snorted, knowing that would be a miracle since they were in a drought.

Yes, her father had built this place safe, and if Lilly got out of this alive, the first place she would go was the hospital in search for her father.

Chapter Three

He came riding on the beast he called his metal horse. His gaze claimed her the first time he saw her. Her Dark Knight, who would show his White Lilly the light.

Dark Horse, Enforcer of the White Buffalo MC

Dark Horse took a drink of his beer, scanning the bar around him. They had arrived at the hotel ten minutes ago. Checking in, he had come straight to the bar, needing a beer and to think. Next to him, Sun Bull sat, both of them saying nothing. Every time before they went out to risk their lives they would sit quietly, watching their little part of their world around them.

But, it would seem, Running Wolf's Little Gypsy had a different idea as she ran into the bar, scanning the little place. "I swear that woman is going to get herself killed," Dark Horse growled as she approached their table.

Kizzy placed a piece of paper in front of Dark Horse. "You have to come upstairs, now," she pleaded as he lifted the paper reading the email.

"My Lilly sent this?" He scooted his chair back just as Running Wolf came into the bar.

"Kizzy!" he growled, coming up to her and yanking her head back by a handful of her hair. "What do you think you were doing? Running out of our room without protection."

"I had to. I was worried about Lilly." Kizzy had tears in her eyes.

"I'm sorry."

Running Wolf moaned. "Little Gypsy, you have to start thinking before you take off. Now, what is so important you risk coming here?"

"Her email was hacked, they know we're coming, and they know Lilly contacted us. She could be in more danger, but Running Wolf, he knew about us and our little girl..." Kizzy's voice cracked...

"How do you know this?"

"This isn't the only email I got. Another one arrived right after this one, from a different address. From someone named Fizz...and the pictures he sent." She shivered rubbing her arms.

"Let's go. I want to see everything. But, Kizzy, Running Wolf is right. I know you were upset, but you should have told Running Wolf about this before coming down here. We're too close for you to be running around without protection..." Dark Horse restated what his friend had just told her, coming around and placing a kiss on the top of her head. "Thank you, little sister, for worrying. But allow us to handle this, please."

"You don't understand, those pictures," she whispered, a tear rolling down her cheek before she buried her face into Running Wolf's chest. Even though, Kizzy wasn't his woman Dark Horse's stomach clenched. He hated to see a woman cry. Unless, of course, it was a good cry, from the punishment he liked to dish out.

"Come, let's take this upstairs. I don't trust anyone around us." Running Wolf led Kizzy out of the bar, followed by Dark Horse, and up to their room.

'Dark Horse stared at the pictures Kizzy handed him anger simmering deep inside.

This Fuzz, president of the Irons—there would be no mercy for him when he got hold of him. But what drew his attention was the hurt, and pain in his woman's eyes. The ache inside his chest, the need to protect her was so strong it even surprised him.

After opening the email for their group, Dark Horse typed his warning then sent it out.

I heard being skinned alive and fed to an army of fire ants is an extremely painful way to die. Get ready. I'm coming for you.

He hit send before opening another email to her.

My White Lilly,
Stay safe. We are coming. Before you know it, you'll be walking out in the sun where you belong.
Dark Horse

He sent the email off, short and the truth. He'd make sure his Lilly was always safe. No way she would be running around free like his little sister, Kizzy, without getting her cute ass spanked. Dark Horse tilted his head, listening to Kizzy's cries, knowing Running Wolf was taking his hand to her backside.

He was just about ready to close the laptop when, another email popped up, from her. Dark Horse smiled and opened it.

I have no idea who you are, but I'm not your anything. I'm safe for now, but they are searching for me. And for your information, I was never White Lilly, just Lilly.
Good night, Dark Horse. You stay safe.

The computer dinged again, and he growled seeing who it was from. This policeman would be second on his list, he promised himself as he opened up the email, seeing a house burning to the ground.

I'll find her and when I do, I'll make sure nothing is left for you.

The threat had him clutching the laptop, standing, and slowly closing the lid. It was time to go, now.

In his hotel room, Dark Horse opened his duffel bag and prepared himself. A calmness seemed to settle over him, knowing every action now affected his Lilly.

Running Wolf entered, wearing his leather and weapons.

"I take it Kizzy's uncle and brother are with her and the baby?" Dark Horse slipped into his coat.

"Yes," he replied. "You didn't inform her we were going in tonight, did you?"

"I'm not stupid. Any word on the scouts?" He glanced around his room one more time, ready to go.

"Yes, they are expecting us to come in on the main road." Running Wolf moved into the hallway Dark Horse followed. At least twenty-five of their men waited in the hallway. The rest would be below waiting on their bikes.

"Thank you everyone for helping me with this. May the great spirit watch your back and the Mother guide your steps." went down the stairs to get on Flames, his metal horse. They had two hours of driving before they would hide their bikes. Already, their scouts were disposing of the Irons' scouts. The Irons wouldn't expect them tonight, but tomorrow, their mistake.

He glanced up, seeing the stars and Father Moon bright in the sky as he opened his horse up and rode down the road, his best friends at his side. Tonight, the Irons would fall.

All the training of the old came back to him in a rush as he climbed off his bike at their destination and crawled to the ridge overlooking the town below. Next to him Running Wolf and Sun Bull, used sign language or as they called it, hand talking, in case there were any recording devices around. Loud music emanated from the party below

Hoots in the night air let him know the enemy scouts were no longer a problem. Dark Horse raised his hand; it was time. As he made his way toward the town, the first two groups, one coming in from the north and the other coming in from the south, started moving in, careful of the townspeople. The first Iron Dark Horse came across was in the single alley in town. Two bikers had dragged a young teenager, screaming as they stripped her of clothes, slapping her around before he could get to her. But they hadn't had time to rape her like they had his lady, Dark Horse growled, shoving his knife in one of the men from behind, twisting it causing as much damage as possible before yanking the blade out and greeting the other biker as the dead man fell at his feet.

"You should really have a willing participant, but then again, who would want to fuck a scumbag like you," Dark Horse taunted.

"Let's dance, Tonto," he snarled and charged Dark Horse who been waiting, and stabbed his new knife into the man's throat. The blade, sharp enough to cut through tin, sliced through his skin without a problem, silencing his words forever as he crumpled next to his friend.

Dark Horse apologized to the Great Mother for taking two of her children then he heard the whimpers of the young girl. Tucking his knife away, Dark Horse kicked the dead man out of his way and knelt next to the girl.

"I won't hurt you." He pointed to the opposite end of the alley. "If you go that way, you will have a clear path, but do not stay in town." He took off his coat and slipped off his shirt, handing it to her. "Here, put this on, little one. It will cover you till you get home. I suggest you stay there tonight. Lock the doors. I'm hoping this will all be over by tomorrow."

The girl turned around to put it on. "Thank you." She glanced back at him. "I'm Emma. Watch for the sheriff and his men. They give them anything they want." Her gaze dropped to the ground. "Even me."

"It will stop tonight. Just stay hidden, little Emma." He put his coat back on and headed toward town from which shouts could be heard. Fighting had begun.

"Sir?" the little girl called, and he glanced over his shoulder at her. "My father is being held in the jail. He's all I have."

"Do you have a place to hide till this is over?"

She turned toward the woods. "Yes, but how long should I stay there?"

"Stay the night there. I promise tomorrow will be better." He smiled at the teenager. She would defiantly attract the boys. "Does your father know where this place is?"

She nodded, inching toward the woods.

"Good, when I see him, I'll tell him. Stay safe, little Emma," he told her, moving out of the alleyway toward the fighting, intent on finding this Fuzz. Running Wolf moved in, and joined him, followed, a few seconds later by Sun Bull.

"It's a good night. The Great Mother has blessed us this

evening. So far not one of ours have gone down," Sun Bull's voice was strong and loud as all three of them stopped and stared at the twenty Iron members waiting for them. But Dark Horse's attention was only for the man in the back.

"Fuzz is mine," Dark Horse informed his friends.

"The sheriff is mine," Running Horse announced next.

"Well, damn, I guess I get to take the one who keeps touching his dick. Maybe he has crabs." Sun Bull's comment was loud enough for the Irons to hear.

Dark Horse snorted, and Running Wolf laughed while said Iron man charged with the others, but the White Buffalos were not alone. All sixty of Running Wolf's men moved up behind them.

***

Lilly sat up, her heart racing a mile a minute as she scanned everything around her. Releasing the breath, she was holding, Lilly's heartbeat slowed and her pulse lowered. She was still safe, but a quick peek up at one of the monitors it was still dark. What had woken her up?

A movement, off to her left, on one of the many little monitors on the ceiling, but that wasn't the only one. Lilly moved closer and sucked in her breath.

"They're here," she whispered, watching the fighting in the middle of town.

The White Buffalo's fought as a team, each anticipating the others' moves. Fuzz stared the line of men his.

Her gaze jumped to the man in the long black leather coat with a White Buffalo on the back of it. He was taller than the rest, but what had her staring were the knives he pulled out as the group of Irons rushed them. One by one, the Iron bikers fell, blood seemed to coat the street where they fought.

His men losing, Fuzz wasn't about to stick around. He and two of his men dashed in between two buildings and met the sheriff. They jumped into a black Blazer and took off.

Her hands shook as the Blazer came to a stop. Would they turn toward her home or head out of town? Lilly grabbed onto the table in front of her as the ground shook beneath her. "Fuck not again," she cried. The large ravine that had surrounded her home was gone on one side. Anyone with a car or bike could now come onto her property, which also meant one could search till they found her.

Lilly quickly ran to the stairs and turned on the light to stare at the metal door. "Will you hold against them?" She trembled, really afraid all of a sudden. "Fuck." As Lilly scanned each camera, a single tear rolled down her cheek.

The Blazer was gone. She had no idea where the four most dangerous men had gone.

"Okay, Daddy. I hope that door is bullet and dynamite proof," she whispered. In the next few hours, her world was going to change, but was it going to be for the good, or would she die that tonight? Lilly moved back to the sofa', hugging herself as she stared at the monitor of the town where all the fighting had taken place.

Never did she take her eyes off the one that seemed to draw her attention. He now stood, with his head bowed, his knives still in his hand's as if saying a prayer, before lifting his head and turning sideways. Lilly swore he stared at the hidden camera, and his dark eyes didn't seem to move for a few seconds, as if he was calling to her in some way.

Two of his friends came to his side, one having a cut on his arm, drawing Dark Horse's attention. Oh, Lilly had known it was Dark Horse. The one who claimed she was his in the email. Plus, he was also the man in her dreams. She scooted back on the sofa, bringing her knees up and hugging them. What did she have to offer a man like that? Could she even allow another to touch her after what had been done to her?

Sure, the nurse inside Lilly knew it wasn't her fault. She'd been raped and taken by at least four of the Irons. But it still didn't stop her from shaking and wanting to rip her skin off her body every time she thought of their rape. The first time was the worst. After that, Lilly had numbed to their groping. Silently crying while they took her body, she'd retreated inside herself.

"Are you going to be able to break through the barrier, my Dark Warrior?" she whispered, curling up on the sofa watching as the townsfolk slowly came out of their houses. Peeking to see what was going on.

But what was really freaky was that the bodies of dead Iron men seem to sink into the ground where they lay. That nothing, not even the blood that had once stained the streets was there. As if the Earth was getting rid of what was toxic to this world.

"What the hell?" she whispered for the first time noticing that the blacktop was gone. There was no paved road coming into town. A dirt road was there now. Several women bent to where the road had been and ran their fingers over the ground.

"Okay, *Twilight Zone* is in full force here," she mumbled, returning her attention going to the property around her burnt-down house.

"What?" She sat up straight as a van, truck, and a few other cars pulled into her drive over the lump that had once been the ravine. A tall, older man, rode up and seemed to be scanning the area, before he nodded, moving his horse closer to where the door to her underground hideout was.

"I know you can hear me, child. You're safe now. My warriors surround your home. You can come out, Lilly," he yelled, as a woman climbed out of the van, carrying a tiny little bundle in her arms. Four men hovered around her, one seemed to be yelling, but she ignored him moving up to the old Native American man.

"Is she here?" she asked.

"She is, but will this Lilly have the courage to come out now?" the man almost challenged her.

Lilly peered down at herself and sighed. She looked like shit, but there was nothing she could do about that. Throwing off her T-shirt, Lilly slid on the sun dress she had found' among the things her father left for her. At the bottom of the stairs, she took a deep breath and reached over, flipping the lock mechanism.

At first, Lilly didn't know if it would work, but after a few groans and clicks, two of men who had surrounded the woman above opened the door and peeked inside her little safe haven.

"Hello, I'm Stephan Lala. We're not here to hurt you, but to help you. You sent an email to my niece, Kizzy." He nodded to the woman with the child.

Kizzy pushed the man out of her way and came down a few steps. "Wow, this place is amazing. Do you mind if I, well, we come in? I'm Running Wolf's wife. The one who's most likely i going to get her butt tanned for coming here. But I didn't want you to be thrust into another bunch of bikers on your own. I know how scary that can be."

"Please. I'm afraid it's not much." She stepped aside as Kizzy moved the rest of the way down the stairs followed by the man who had been on the horse.

"Yes, your father did a fine job here. By the way he is well, just needs a few more days with the doctors and you'll have him by your side again. My name is Soaring Eagle." He bowed his head.

"He has a gift or two and knows things." Kizzy tilted her head to the side. "You have a small one, too, don't you, Lilly"

Lilly shrugged and moved to fridge to get some water. She offered one to Kizzy.

"No thank you, I have some in the van."

"You do know the leader of the Irons is still roaming around with the sheriff and two others, right?" Lilly watched their reaction.

Kizzy smiled, sitting down on the sofa before putting her sleeping baby next to her. "It won't matter. They can't get through the warriors out there. Dark Horse and Running Wolf have ordered this place protected, knowing you were here somewhere."

Lilly pulled out a folding chair and nodded to the older man. "Please, sit." She pointed to the other chairs as the two other males moved down the stairs to join them.

"Lilly the man on the right is my older brother, Mason, and the other one my uncle, Stephan. Have you heard anything?" Kizzy rubbed her daughters back.

"The town is clear, but still no sight of the sheriff or the president of the Irons. Running Wolf did manage to find a few of the deputies and have them locked in their own cell, waiting for his friend who should arrive here tomorrow or the next day." Mason smiled at her. "It's a pleasure to finally meet you, Lilly. Kizzy has been really worried about you."

Kizzy shrugged. "I have a little talent from my mother. I knew you were important to us, to Dark Horse. Plus, no one should go through what you did."

Lilly knew that expression all too well. It was one she saw every day when she stared into the mirror. "It happened to you, too?".

Kizzy smiled, but it was a sad one. "Once, but it was enough, especially since it was with someone I thought was special."

A growl came from the stairs. "And when were you going to tell me about this?" Running Wolf pushed into the crowded room. "Why don't we take this up top, it's safe and you, you're supposed to be at the hotel where I left you. His hair was wet and he wore different pants.

Kizzy handed him the baby and pushed past him, holding out her hand. "Are you ready to face a new day?"

Lilly looked up the stairs and saw him, standing there at the top. His hair was damp, too. He wore a pair of jeans, black boots, and nothing else, except the feather in his braid.

"They are impressive when they want to be, but, Lilly, he'll never hurt you if you give him a chance." Kizzy hooked her arm with hers. "Ready?" she asked again, and all Lilly could do was nod.

"Wait, do you have shoes? You can't come out here barefoot." The voice above sent a chill down her spine.

She glanced around and found her sandals, slipping them on before moving to the bottom of the stairs with Kizzy. "Ready, I think."

Kizzy took her hand and they climbed to the top of the stairs. The night wind gently blew on her face, but tears flooded her eyes. It was even worse than seeing it on the monitors. Her family home was gone. Nothing but burnt wood, still hot in some spots.

"It's all gone," she whispered, tears rolled down her cheeks, blurring her vision.

"I'm sorry we didn't get here soon enough, my Lilly." Dark Horse scooped her up in his arms. "Those little sandals are not shoes, my woman, and I will not have you getting hurt again."

She stiffened in his arms, but he didn't stop until they were past the debris where he lowered her feet to the ground and brushed the tears off her cheeks. "I really am sorry, Lilly."

"It's not your fault, it's theirs. Plus, you don't even know me." She backed up a step, but that was all he would allow her as his arm still was around her waist.

"No, I don't, but I aim to change that. I'm not leaving." He reached up and tucked a lock of hair behind her ear.

Chapter Four

"Her tears water of the soul, but her smile the light of his."
Dark Horse, Enforcer of the White Buffalo MC

Dark Horse couldn't believe he was actually holding his Lilly, but what had his heart breaking were the tears rolling down her cheeks as she surveyed the total destruction of her family home. Seeing his woman's tears was one of the worst feelings in the world, right up there with his mother's death.

"I'd like to take you back to the hotel we're staying at till we can decide what we are going to do next," he told her softly. "I'll have my men pack up everything in that shelter for you."

She shrugged. "I really would like to go to the hospital and see my father." Lilly's voice was but a whisper.

Dark Horse glanced at Kizzy's uncle. "Do you know the way to the hospital?"

"I'll put it in the GPS. You can follow me," Stephan stood close, scanning around them, always alert.

"Good." Dark Horse turned, watching Running Wolf who place his little baby girl into her car seat. Anger was evident on his face, but Kizzy ignored him and came over to Lilly. "I'm at the hotel, too. We have a room right across from Dark Horse. If you need anything, I don't care what time it is, you come and get me." Lilly reached over and hugged Lilly tight. "You can get through this."

She nodded as Running Wolf came over. "You really should go with us to have that cut checked out. I think it's deep enough to get

41

stitches," Lilly told him.

"Not to worry. Our medic will heal me tonight. Go visit your father. We'll see you both in the morning. Dark Horse, I'm leaving twenty of our men here to follow you two since we still haven't found Fuzz or the sheriff. I don't trust that bastard not to backtrack. He's going to be furious that his men are either dead or locked up."

"Thank you. Are you ready?" Dark Horse said, and she nodded.

He guided her to his bike, where he dug into his saddlebag, pulled out a small leather coat, and handed it to her. "I bought this for you a couple of days ago. I hope it fits. I knew you'd need a riding coat."

Lilly ran her hand over the soft leather. "You bought this for me?"

"I have a few things I've picked up for you. I meant what I told you Lilly. There is something there, and I know it will take time for you to heal. But I have waited for this day." He glanced up at the sky. "I'm not perfect. I have my dark side, but I always will tell you the truth, no matter how much it hurts. I only ask the same from you."

"Why didn't anyone come help us?" Her red puffy eyes stared up at him. "We've been under attack here over a month, and not one person came in and helped us. Only you did." She slid the coat on.

"I don't know why, Lilly." Reaching over, he zipped the coat up. "Fate's way for us to meet. But then it might have something to do with the sheriff and his deputies. We'll figure it out, but for now try not to worry. I know it's hard to trust us, but we really are here to help." He kept the other half of their story to himself for now.

He got onto his metal horse, waiting as Lilly climbed on behind him.

"I know there's more, but thank you for all of this, including the coat. It's beautiful, but I have no way to pay you back Dark Horse. Hell, I don't even know if I have my money in my back account anymore." She wrapped her arms around him as he started his bike.

"Hold on. Take these," Running Wolf yelled, coming over and handing them two helmets.

Dark Horse groaned, but knew it was best. Plus, he'd be able to talk to her as they rode. "Thank you. Didn't even think of these."

"Don't mention it. You'll get used to them. Plus, you had no problem on the way here talking with us. Be careful, both of you." Running Wolf turned, moving back to the van. Even though his outward appearance appeared normal, Dark Horse had seen the small twitch of his eye. Yes, Kizzy and he would be having a long, long chat after her ass was red.

"Was something wrong with your friend?" She took the helmet and put it on.

Dark Horse reached over and flipped on the microphone, removing his feather and tucking it in his coat before donning his helmet. "Kizzy never should have been here. She should have stayed at the hotel with their daughter where they would have been safe."

"I believe she was just trying to help me. You know, seeing another woman."

Dark Horse pulled out onto the road following Kizzy's uncle. For some strange reason, the man had formed a kind of bond with him.

Lily rested her head against his back. "I'm a registered nurse. I know all the signs of a women who has been raped, and so does Kizzy. She knew another female would help with the fear, and she was right. Even her little girl helped some, the innocent helping to sooth the one burned," she told him, her voice almost on auto pilot.

"This world is changing, Lilly. It's going to be a more dangerous time. We'll be reverting back to a lot of the old ways to survive. With this we expect, no I will demand, you listen for your own safety. I know this sounds barbaric, but I won't lose you. Running Wolf lost Kizzy for a minute when her enemies attacked her. I will not allow that to happen to you now that I've found you."

What he wasn't expecting was his woman's laugh, a downright sexy one, too, which had his cock hardening in his jeans.

"You are too much. First, we just met. Second, I haven't even agreed to any of this between us, so you need pull in the reins, my Dark Warrior, because right now tonight I'm on the verge of busting down. And I sure don't want that to happen in front of my father."

Dark Horse didn't say anything, allowing his silence to be his answer, until they pulled into the hospital parking lot. He turned off his bike. At once, Lilly was off the bike and heading toward the hospital, but Dark Horse reached out and pulled her back into his arms, taking her helmet off. He placed it on her seat, turning his gaze on her.

"I'm sorry my words were rough, but as I told you, I won't lie. I know you can feel the connection, and I won't call you on it right now. I agree you have been through a nightmare situation, and I'd give anything you hadn't been. But that does not change the fact you are still in danger, my little flower." He cupped her cheek. "Please, for my peace of mind, try and listen to what I say?" He glanced behind her and nodded to Stephan who waited for them. "Now we can go. It's safe."

Lilly sighed. "It's really not over, is it?"

The fear and tears in her eyes broke his heart. Dark Horse took her hands into his. "My Lilly, I'm not perfect, and I know we'll butt heads, but I've done this before. Please trust me to keep you safe. The rest, we'll go slow."

"I can't promise you anything." She took a deep breath. "You know what hurt worst?" Lilly peered over her shoulder at him as he stood. "Knowing my father had to watch them take me and could do nothing." Lilly gazed up at the hospital. "He already felt as if he didn't do enough for my mother, when she was sick, but now..." Lilly shook her head and moved forward as he kept pace next to her, always scanning their surroundings, even when they moved into the hospital.

"I can't imagine having a daughter and watching that happen. But he is alive, and I bet right now his only concern is seeing his baby safe." Dark Horse pushed the elevator button for them. Stephan had already found out what room her father was in.

Lilly stepped into the empty elevator. "What floor do they have him on?"

Stephan grunted and pushed the number eight button. "The cardiac floor. Your father had three stints put in yesterday but is in good condition otherwise. We will have a few men watching his room, along with the state police, since it's obvious no one around here can trust your local department of police."

Dark Horse glanced at Stephan. "I take it Running Wolf contacted his friends with the Federal Bureau?"

"Yes, and from what we found out, not only this city, but the next one over is corrupt as hell. Running Wolf has men watching them, thinking the sheriff will go there."

"How many men there?" Dark Horse didn't like this news. It could mean trouble.

"With the police force and a few men of the Irons who got away,

I'm thinking at least twenty, but we'll be ready." Stephan stepped out onto the eighth floor when the door opened.

Lilly went to move around him, but Dark Horse held onto her. "Always allow the guards to go first to make sure no one is waiting for you." Dark Horse nodded to Stephan. "When he gives the okay, we follow."

"Are you telling me I'm going to have a guard on me?" Lilly glanced from Stephan to Dark Horse.

Stephan smiled and shook his head as he moved down the corridor. Dark Horse sighed. "Yes, Lilly, there is more than you know going on here. I'll explain after you get some rest and food in you. But for now, let's go see your father." Dark Horse guided her to the room.

"Now you've really got me curious." Lilly stopped and took a deep breath as they stood there before her father's door.

Dark Horse rubbed her back. "Right now, just seeing you will help him."

She nodded and pushed open the door'. One of Running Wolf's men sat guarding him. The others waited out in the hall.

"Daddy," Lilly cried and ran to her father, hugging him tight. Tears rolled down their cheeks as they just held each other, till her father lifted his head and stared straight at him.

"So, you are the man who rescued my Lilly. The one who will keep her safe for the rough times coming our way?" Darvin, asked, his voice deep and strong for a man who just had a major heart attack.

"I am." Dark Horse moved into the room and held out his hand to Lilly's father.

Lilly held onto to her father but turned a little to watch as Dark Horse shook his hand. The way he was staring at Dark Horse had her squirming. "Daddy, when are they going to release you?"

Instead of answering he asked his own question, sending a shiver up her spine. "How long do we have?"

"It's already started in some spots around the world. Our best guess, two, maybe three years," Dark Horse answered.

"Wait, what are you talking about?" Lilly looked at her father then back to Dark Horse.

Her father arched a brow. "You haven't explained things to her yet?"

"Sir, we just met, and your daughter has been through an emotional and physical trauma. I'd like to give her some time before I load her down with everything going on around us."

"Um, excuse me. Anyone going to answer my question?" Lilly was getting a little pissed off.

"Calm down, princess," her father scolded. "I get to leave in two days if everything comes back okay with the tests. Now, where are you going to stay tonight? I take it the house is gone?"

Lilly heard the pain in his voice. "I'm sorry, Daddy. There was nothing I could have done." She got up and moved around his man, going to the window. "As soon as the ground opened up around the house, Fuzz..." She shivered and rubbed her hands up and down on her arms, but Dark Horse pushed her hands away, pulling her into his arms, his warmth.

"He got mad he couldn't get to you and burned the house down, not caring if you were in it," Dark Horse snarled.

She glanced over her shoulder at Dark Horse. Where Fuzz was a bully, rapist, and a downright nasty man, this one was quiet, deadly, a true warrior.

Lilly couldn't help but smile. "Do you take scalps?"

He smiled. "Actually, the white man started that tradition, but believe me I know many different old ways. This Fuzz better hope the Great Mother takes him because I won't be so kind." He cupped her cheek. "No one touches what is mine."

'She slowly turned around to face her father. "Why are you smiling, Daddy? We don't even know him." She nodded to Dark Horse as she slid out his arms, knowing he had allowed her to escape.

"Because I knew he was coming. I've seen you two together, princess. He is your destiny, even if you don't want to see it right now, but he will give you the time you need."

"Of course. I've already told your daughter it will take time for her to trust me and my men, but we will get there. Have you had any contact with the local tribes here?" Dark Horse answered.

Her father shook his head. "But I know they have a few reservations here in Texas. Your best bet would be to contact them through May-Run. He's missing, but I have a feeling he's hunting the Irons. I heard the president yelling about men he can't locate. Maybe it was him. who knows. But if it was, he'll contact you soon enough."

"Not to change the subject here, but how long have you been building that safe place? Why didn't we know you've been updating it and such?" Lilly sat on the side of his bed.

"Remember when they came to work on our sewer?"

"That was years ago, and wait, wouldn't the idiot who dug the sewer have known what you were doing?" Lilly growled, thinking of the ass who had later joined with the Irons, wrecking the town and raping young girls.

Her father frowned. "You don't like Jason?"

"You're kidding, right? He raped at least three of our teens, vandalized the general store, and stood there watching Fuzz..." Lilly's stomach knotted, and she jumped up, moving away from her father and the men. "No, Father, he's just as bad if not worse than them. A few men from our town seemed to snap, joining in on their destruction and rape, not caring about those they lived around for years." She looked back at her father. "You wouldn't recognize some of our neighbors, I'm afraid."

He scooted up in the bed, frowning at her. "I don't understand. How could these men turn on our women?"

Dark Horse frowned. "I'm afraid there are some who hide what they would love to do, but when a person like this Fuzz comes along...Well, they open a new opportunity for them to do what they have dreamed of, thinking that nothing will happen to them now. It's sad, but I'm afraid our society has forgotten what it is to be civil to those around them. Maybe this is another reason why the Great Mother has had enough. Too much blood soaking into the Earth."

"Do you really believe this?" Lilly asked.

He turned his gaze on her. "Yes. The cruelty I have seen over the years has grown to an alarming rate. Racism, hate, and depraved individuals are far too common now. It's an everyday event in our world. We've become accustomed to hearing it in the news."

"I think most people just ignore it or turn off the source, but you are right on some aspects." Lilly shook her head. "Even working in the ER, I see so many teenagers who think the world owes them. That they don't have to work for anything. Take, take, take. That is all they think about. I call it the me generation. It's all about them, nothing else, and if you get in their way watch out. Spoiled brats whose parents could care less as long as they are not in their hair."

A nurse, Cleo, came into the room. "I'm sorry, but visiting hours are almost up." She turned to her. "Are you okay? We've all been worried about you ever since your father told us what was happening. We tried to call in the state police, but every time we did, nothing happened." She hugged Lilly. Her colleague stepped back and stared at her, and Lilly couldn't help but look away.

Cleo drew in a sharp breath. "Do you need to be tested, Lilly?"

Lilly nodded. God knew what kind of diseases she had gotten from them. "Please."

"Come. I'll do it myself and make sure Dr. Morree gives you the antibiotics you'll need just to be on the safe side," Cleo started to pull her out of the room, but Dark Horse came up from behind her, wrapping his arm around her, stopping all movement.

"She goes nowhere without me or her guard. The Irons are still roaming about, and they will be aiming for Lilly." Dark Horse stared down at her. "Do you need to do this now?"

"Yes, this shouldn't wait. If by any chance they gave me something..." Lilly's eyes filled with tears as she glanced away from the handsome man who held her.

"It's not your fault. Remember that. Now, we'll go, but I will guard the room so no one comes in." Dark Horse placed a kiss on the top of her head. "No one will hurt you again, Lilly." He tried to reassure her, again, but for some strange reason Lilly had a feeling this was far from over.

She went to her father's bedside, leaning down hugging, him tight. "I love you, Daddy. I'll be here to pick you up. We'll figure out what we're going to do next, together."

"I'll be waiting for you both." He grabbed her chin and lifted her head up till his gaze met hers. "You can trust him, Lilly. I've seen it. We have a long, hard road ahead of us, but we must stay strong. You now have that man to lean on, to help you. Don't close up, little flower." He kissed her forehead. "Now, go get your medicine and tests so you can get some good sleep."

She glanced back at Dark Horse standing there staring at her. Lilly swore he could see everything she was thinking. The way he watched her every move was a little intimidating, but she had always wanted a relationship like her parents'. She stood straight, patting her dad's shoulder, remembering the way he always took care of her mom. "He's like you, isn't he?"

Her father smiled. "It's what you need. Just like your dear mother. I miss her so much. She balanced me, and I feel you will do this for your man. I've explained this to you, Lilly. Like your mother, you need guidance and a strong hand. There is nothing wrong with this."

"I'm not a child, Dad. I'm an emergency room nurse. I deal with life and death every day," she mumbled.

"And you handle that fine, but when it comes to your own life, that is where you need the help, no?"

Lilly fidgeted for a moment until Dark Horse's hands settled on her shoulders, squeezing them. "I will always be there for you, my Lilly. We must go. Your friend is waiting for us, and we have a drive back to the hotel yet." Dark Horse patted her father's shoulder. "We will be here as soon as the doctor gives us the word you are able to be discharged. I'm leaving two men here, and federal agents are coming in to help us, so you should be fine. My man has also spoken with hospital security."

"Thank you, and please take care of our flower. She's all I have left of her mother and means the world to me." Her father's words brought tears to her eyes as Dark Horse guided her out of the room, following Cleo who kept glancing between her and Dark Horse.

"Relax, Cleo. He truly did save the town, him and his friends. I'd still be there if it wasn't for them," Lilly told her.

They moved through the doors to the unit she knew so well, ER. At once, her friends rushed her, hugging and crying as they all talked.

Lilly laughed and brushed tears away. "God I missed you three. Arnina, Hayley, Kiana, I'd like to introduce my hero, Dark Horse. He and his friends saved our town and me." She pointed behind her as her friends had surrounded her.

He snorted and shook his head as Kizzy's uncle moved up next to him.

"Well, it seems like you'll have plenty of nurses to help you." He nudged Dark Horse, who grunted.

"Ladies it's a pleasure to meet you all. I hate to rush this, but Lilly really needs to get some sleep, so if we could hurry this up so I can get her to the hotel, please?" Dark Horse placed his hand on her back.

Dr. Morree approached them. "Don't you think it would be wise if she stayed with one of her friends?"

All of her friends moaned as the doctor went into protective mode.

"Dr. Morree, I'm fine, and Dark Horse? Well..." Lilly faltered.

"I'm going to marry Lilly. There is no safer place than next to me," Dark Horse growled then pulled her into his side.

Chapter Five

"His dark eyes captured hers. The declaration that she was to marry him sent her into an anger fit, but, inside, her soul rejoiced, knowing she'd met her match."

Lilly

"You're going to what? I just met you three hours ago?" his woman sputtered, making him smile right before he covered her mouth with his. Tasting everything that was his flower. He nipped her bottom lip, waiting for the moment when she opened her mouth then sliding in, their tongues dancing to a hidden song in their heads. She tasted of mint, no doubt the toothpaste she had used.

Not wanting to push too fast, when all he wanted to do was lay her out on the floor and explore every aspect of the body he'd worship for the rest of his life, Dark Horse broke away from her, allowing her to escape him. "Go, Lilly. Your friend is waiting for you. I'll be right out here, little flower." He turned her around and slapped her ass.

Dark Horse leaned against the wall next to the door to the examining room, Stephan next to him.

"That is one brave woman you have there. I got word from my brother. T president wasn't the only one who raped her. She's going to need a gentle hand." Stephan glanced at him.

"Are you warning me, or is this Kizzy?" he growled.

"Both. I've seen firsthand what rape can do to a woman. It's a long battle you two will have to face together." Stephan squeezed his arm. "But I have confidence in you. I'll call the hotel and make sure some food is ready for you when you get there. She needs a good meal, bath, and sleep right now."

"Thank you, Stephan, and I know the problems as well. A number of our women were attacked on the reservations, my mom for one."

Stephan headed for the parking lot, pulling out his phone as he went.

Dark Horse glanced at the door. Everything in him wanted to push it open and join her, but she was still nervous around him. Plus, Cleo was bound and determined to speak with her alone, just to make sure he wasn't forcing Lilly.

For that alone, he'd make sure her friends were with them when they set up the safe place. The door next to him creaked open, and Lilly poked her head out. "Um, I know we don't know each other well, but could you..."

"Little flower, I'll do anything I can for you." He entered the room.

Lilly held the paper gown closed, as she got up on the table, scooting down to the edge as the doctor came into the room. "I wanted him to come in, Dr. Morree."

The doctor nodded and moved to the end of the table as Lilly, held her hand out to Dark Horse. Something settled inside him as he took her hand, leaning against the table, giving her as much support as he could. Dark Horse placed a kiss on the top of her head. "I'm here, little flower. Why don't you tell me about yourself? What is your favorite color? Do you like Mexican food? Do you like spice in your food?" He whispered, the last part in her ear, nipping it.

She slapped his arm. "Behave." She giggled. "My favorite color is blue, like the sky. I love Mexican, but my stomach can't tolerate the spiciness of some of the food. Also, I love Chinese. I love to cook."

The doctor snorted. "She's a baker. Half of us have gained at least five pounds on her sweets she brings in here. You're going to feel me, now, Lilly. We'll be done in a minute."

She squeezed his hand, staring up at him. Her bottom lip trembled, and tears formed in her eyes. Fire ants. He needed to find some because this Fuzz was going to suffer when he got hold of him.

He knelt next to her. "When I was a kid, my mom had a hell of a time with me. I was twelve when I decided I needed to see if a bull would go after anything with the color red. I dressed in my red shirt and shorts and jumped into the tribe's pasture. I swear it wasn't even five minutes when I had two bulls coming for me, chasing me. The only reason I'm standing here is because one of the warriors who was taking care of the herd came to my rescue. Needless to say, I couldn't sit for the next two days, Mom was so furious."

Her eyes got big and her lips twitched, right before she burst out laughing. "Oh my god, your poor mom," she cried as her friend Cleo snorted.

"It must be a boy thing because I swear my son would do that if there were bulls any around." Cleo drew two tubes of blood.

"Hey, I resent that." Dr. Morree stood. "All done, Lilly. I'll get your prescription ready, but..." He glanced at him. "For now, use protection till we know."

Dark Horse nodded, not wanting to embarrass his woman any more than necessary. He took a step back, but Lilly's grip on his hand grew tighter. "I'm not going anywhere. Just going to grab your clothes for you." He cupped her cheek, waiting for to take a breath.

"Okay." Lilly released his hand.

"Lilly, why don't you go wash up in the bathroom. By the time you get dressed, I'll have the meds for you." Cleo followed the doctor out of the room.

Lilly slid off the table and into the bathroom where he placed her pants and under garments. "I'll be right here by the door," Dark Horse told her as she closed the door partway, leaving it cracked so she could see him.

"So, tell me about this thing that is going to happen, that Dad was talking about. It will help keep my mind busy." Lilly wouldn't give up.

Dark Horse sighed. "There are signs among our people that the dark times are coming. Already a few cities have been destroyed. It was only a matter of time before the Great Mother took back the Earth, since we are destroying it at a fast rate. Soaring Eagle, our medicine man, believes we have a few years before this happens. He, too, sees things and has told us to set up four large bases to help those around for these times. One such base will be here. You and I will be setting it up, getting ready. I have twenty men who will be staying with us. But I also want to get the other tribes in the area to help."

The door opened, and Lilly stepped out of the bathroom. "Why just Native Americans? Are you prejudiced against my race?" She gave him a look that had him smiling.

"Far from it, little flower." He reached out and pulled her into his arms. "We are taught at an early age the old ways, how to survive when everything fails. Are your people?"

Lilly sighed and rested her forehead on his chest. "No, but do you really believe this is going to happen?"

"It already has. Where Kizzy was living, Milan, Ohio, it's all gone. The Mother took back that land and a few other towns have also disappeared. Even in your there have been changes, no?"

She frowned and tilted her head to the side. "I don't know how or why, but the ground opened up around my house before you came. It was as if someone was protecting me. Fuzz and the others couldn't get to me. Oh, they tried, but a few of them died as the ground further separated. When you came, the ground shifted, closing the hole."

"I'm afraid all of your house is gone, little flower. Even the little space underground. Some of the roads coming to the town are gone. My people are moving your townsfolk to a place nearby, where Soaring Eagle says it will be safe. We have a lot of work ahead of us."

She furrowed her brow. "I'd like to check on a few of the locals tomorrow, especially a few older people. I haven't been in the town for the past two weeks. I don't know what happened to some of them."

"I too have to check on a girl. I caught two men trying to force themselves on her. I want to make sure she and her father are okay. He rubbed his cheek on the top of her head. "Her name is Emma. Pretty little thing, but so innocent."

Lilly stepped back. "Dark hair, small, a pug nose?"

He nodded.

"Oh, my God, no. They have been through so much lately. She is so trusting, Dark Horse. This is going to crush her," His Lilly shook her head, placing her hands on his chest.

"Sort of like you?"

"Well, maybe a little, but she's so young. There are a few of the teens I'd like to check on if it's okay with you. Maybe I can help, if they know I went through what they did."

Dark Horse could see the wheels turning. "You, my lady, amaze me. No wonder you are a nurse. Always wanting to help others even when you are hurting. But we will do this together." He tucked her under his arm and escorted her out of the room, where Cleo met them with pills and some paperwork.

"Here is your medication. I need a phone number where we can reach you when the results come in." Cleo said.

Dark Horse pulled out the phone they had set up last week. He would thank Kizzy later for the idea. "Not too much into phones and this one is new, but here" He handed it to Lilly who scrolled through the phone before giving Cleo a number.

After hugs, and promises to keep in touch, Dark Horse walked a quiet Lilly out of the hospital to his bike where others waited for them.

"Dark Horse, am I going to be able to keep my job?"

He handed her a helmet. "Until we find the other men, I'd prefer you stayed with me. Plus, I believe your talent will be used more useful helping the townspeople, and I'll need your help setting up our camp. You know this area. Would it really bother you not to go back to the hospital?" He needed to know where her head was.

Lilly glanced over her shoulder. "I love the people there, but I've been thinking of leaving the ER for a while now. After two years there, you get kind of burned out. I've lasted the longest, so I think a long break would be welcome." She turned back to him. "But, you're right. Helping my town is important. We're all going to need to lean on each other and I'm afraid even though you and your men helped free them, they're still going to be closed up to you from everything that has happened."

"I agree. It's one of the reason's you and your father will help a lot." He smiled. "I can't wait for you to get to know Soaring Eagle. He's sort of a mentor-father figure for me. I'm going to hate seeing him leave when Running Wolf heads toward Canada." He shook his head, getting onto the bike. "Sorry, I didn't mean to say that." She didn't need to know about his insecurities. Right now, his flower needed to concentrate on herself.

Lilly stared at the strong man before her as he placed the helmet on his head and starting the bike. He did have a weakness, and it was this Soaring Eagle person. Swinging her leg over the bike, she wrapped her arms around him.

"Maybe ask him to stay?" Lilly asked.

He shook his head. "No, he's committed to Kizzy and Running Wolf. I guess each of us has a soft spot for Soaring Eagle. He's been a part of all our lives when we have needed him."

Lilly rested her head against his back. "Then he will see where he is wanted the most, but not to worry. If this connection between us is true, you will have my father and I. Already, my father has given you his blessing, which is strange to say the least since he had never met you."

"Even though I don't know your father, and I don't have a stitch of a gift, he does remind me of Soaring Eagle. I believe they will get along well when they meet." Dark Horse pulled onto the highway heading away from her town.

Surrounded by his men on their bikes, the cool air felt good against her skin. The night stars above seemed to twinkle bright this evening. "You know maybe this is why Soaring Eagle is going with your friend Running Wolf. He sees my father beside you, helping you, us. God, I never realized how much I missed being outside. It's so beautiful, even if it is the middle of the night."

"Don't fall asleep, little flower. I don't want to have to go back and pick you up," Dark Horse teased.

Lilly smiled. "I'm afraid there wouldn't be much there, after everyone ran me over."

"They better not run over my woman," he growled, and Lilly couldn't help but giggle.

"Are you one of those type of men who are very possessive of their women?" Lilly rubbed her cheek against his back, the smell of his leather and the fresh breeze calming her.

"Yes, and I'm also a very jealous man. Just the thought of another touching or even looking at what is mine has my blood warming," he snarled. "I think I'll have to wrap you up tight in a wool blanket, hidden from others."

Lilly did laugh then. "That would itch too much. Plus, how could I share...well, crap, they're all gone. I like fancy lingerie. I had two drawers filled, but it's all gone now." She sighed.

Dark Horse reached down and squeezed her leg. "I'll buy you all new stuff, enough to last years. I'll keep some of it hidden to give to you over the rough times, too."

"You are totally confusing. One minute, I see the old warrior before me, and the next I see a big softy," she teased.

"Only for you, little flower, only for you."

For the next few hours, she and Dark Horse talked about nothing important, he telling her about the White Buffalo's and his life, she sharing about her parents and her life. By the time he pulled up to the hotel, she was stiff from ridding on the bike.

"I think my butt fell asleep," she mumbled, rubbing her ass and stretching when she got off.

"Come here. I'll wake it up." Dark Horse tapped her butt.

"Hey." She laughed and took a step back but didn't get far as his muscular arm brought her back against his side. He escorted her into the hotel with their guard. "How long will we be staying here?"

"Tomorrow, we'll move closer to our destination. Already, we have a few men searching for housing for the next year while we get everything ready for what is to come." They stepped into the elevator of the fancy hotel.

"This is a nice place, little expensive, though."

"You deserve to be pampered for a while, and I aim to see to it." He smiled down at her. "I have a gift for you. I don't know what drew me to it, but I saw it in a window on my way to Texas, and it called to me. I actually got a few things in the antique store. I tried to talk the woman into coming with us, but she wouldn't hear of it."

Lilly patted his chest. "If what you say is true, I'm afraid a lot of people are not going to believe you. All we can do is warn them and help those who will allow us."

The elevator door opened, and Lilly would have stumbled back if Dark Horse didn't have a tight hold on her. There had to be over twenty big men in the hallway waiting, but one man drew her attention.

The same man who had been at her little safe house. Gray hair, skin tanned and wrinkled, he smiled, holding out his hand. "Dark Horse, she is stunning. Yes, your flower will do well beside you. Hello, Lilly. We really didn't get a chance to talk earlier. I'm Soaring Eagle. You are safe here, little girl." He leaned over and placed a kiss on her cheek as Dark Horse and she exited the elevator.

"Thank you. Dark Horse has told me much about you, at least

61

what time allowed. I can't wait to get to know you. But is all this really necessary?" Lilly peered up at him.

"Sorry. I'm afraid the local tribes in the area heard about what happened and have come to offer their support. Dark Horse, I'd like you to meet Black Bull, Seeking Elk, and Raining Song. They represent the majority of the tribes in Texas and will be coordinating with you and the others to start setting up what needs to be done. Gentlemen, this is Dark Horse. He will be the one in charge if you should need anything." Soaring Eagle aid.

Dark Horse glanced at Soaring Eagle, who laughed. "Son, they all know who you are, and their medicine man has seen you coming, so relax," Soaring Eagle placed his hand on Dark Horse's shoulder. "Believe in yourself, because I do. And it's obvious they do, or they wouldn't be here offering their help."

Lilly slid her arm around Dark Horse and squeezed, offering him some support since already he had given her and her father some hope. He turned his dark gaze down at her and winked before reaching out and offering his hand to one of the men, Black Bull, she thought.

"Thank you all for coming tonight and your support. But it is not a good night to discuss what needs to be done. My woman needs to eat and sleep after the hell she had to endure over the last month. I would ask if you or any of your men hear anything of this sheriff..." Dark Horse glanced down at her. "Do you know his name?"

"Sheriff Craig Khan." She shivered then rubbed her arms, but once more Dark Horse wrapped his arms around her, warming her with his body. Lilly didn't know why, but his touch calmed her like nothing else.

One of the men, Seeking Elk glanced at her then at Dark Horse.

"I've heard of this man, and I'm afraid many of our people have had trouble with him and his deputies. I will personally send out word to find him, or any man he's with."

Dark Horse nodded. "That would be appreciated, but Fuzz, the president he is mine. So, if you capture him, hold him. I've waited for two weeks to get hold of this man, and I'll be damned if he escapes the plans I have for him." Dark Horse growled. "Now, if you will excuse us, I want Lilly to soak in a hot tub while I order some food for her."

"Not to worry. Food has been ordered, and Kizzy laid out some clothes for Lilly, knowing she would have very little." Stephan came around the corner, winking at her. "Running Wolf would like to meet everyone in the diner below, tomorrow around noon." Stephan smiled down at her. "He knew you would need sleep, and my niece will have to deal with her punishment tomorrow morning anyway."

"Punishment?" She frowned. "I don't understand."

"I'll explain it to you later. Come." Dark Horse nodded to the men and walked her down the hall, with Soaring Eagle next to them.

"Explain, please," Lilly refused to let it go. After all, the woman had come to help her.

Dark Horse stopped in front of a room and slid the key in. "Our world is become very dangerous as you have seen, Lilly. As I've told you before, I will expect you to obey when I give you an order." He smiled. "Now, I know there will be times when we butt heads, argue, but when it comes to your safety, you will listen or be spanked, and this is not an erotic spanking."

Her face heated, and she glanced down at the floor, knowing Soaring Eagle had heard every word. Now, Lilly wish she had waited till they were alone, damn.

"Not to worry, daughter. My wife felt my hand on her backside many times. God I miss her, but I will be in her arms, soon, when my journey is done."

Dark Horse stiffened. "You know when your journey will be done?"

Soaring Eagle laughed. "Relax, Dark Horse. You will see me again. I will see our new land before I pass. Plus, I want to see the grandchildren you two will be giving me."

"What?" she squeaked.

"I think I saw at least three little girls and two boys. Dark Horse has this thing about seeing his woman round with his child," Soaring Eagle teased.

She shook her head and walked past the two men, smelling delicious food. There were so many different items laid out for them. Sandwiches, steak, chicken, and even ham. Her stomach growled loudly, earning a laugh from behind her.

"Go dig in," Dark Horse told her.

"Aren't you going to eat?" She stared at the food not knowing where to start.

"I will after I clean up, but I'm sure Soaring Eagle will keep you company, since it's obvious he wants to talk so much," Dark Horse grumbled.

"Keep it up, and I'll tell her all about the time you danced with the bull." Soaring Eagle gave him a look her father had down pat.

"Ha, already told her that story," Dark Horse yelled, grabbing a pair of jeans and then going into the bathroom.

"Impressive. He never talks about himself. Eat. I'll join you for a bit, but will leave as soon as Dark Horse comes out." Soaring Eagle grabbed a bottle of water then took a seat at the small table.

"Did Dark Horse happen to tell you about his mother?" Soaring Eagle watched her pile food on her plate.

She joined him at the table. "Only that she passed when he was small." Lilly stuffed a piece of ham into her mouth, moaning.

"Dark Horse knows firsthand what you are going through, daughter. His mother suffered the same fate, but we didn't get to her in time. She died in his arms. Don't get me wrong. Dark Horses mother knew she was dying from cancer, but they took her life when she would have lived a few months more."

"Oh my God. No, he didn't tell me. That's horrible," Lilly glanced at the door where she heard the shower going.

"You have to understand, in our world, many of our women were raped, beaten, and even stolen from us. Who knows? Maybe it's why the Great Mother has alerted us to the changes coming. We've suffered for over a hundred years, from the greedy men who surround us. Men like your Dark Horse have learned to build a shell around themselves. But the Great Mother knew they needed special women to stand beside them, and you are one of those women."

Lilly shook her head. "First, I'm not Dark Horse's woman yet, even if my father approves. Second, I'm nothing special, Soaring Eagle. Sure, I see some things, like my father, but that is nothing. Many people have a déjà thing going on. Third, what or who is the Great Mother?" She took a drink of her diet pop, waiting to hear the story.

Chapter Six

Nature always wears the colors of the spirit.
Ralph Waldo Emerson

Dark Horse listened to Soaring Eagle explain that there were many different Great Spirits in their world. East, West, North, South, heavens, Mother Earth, and, of course, of the soul. He explained even a single object like a rock or the earth we walk on has a soul and can be hurt.

Cleansed of the death that came from his hands, Dark Horse leaned against the bathroom doorframe, watching his woman soak up the knowledge of their world. He had heard Soaring Eagle inform her about his mother and had no problem with Lilly knowing. But it still hurt deep inside that this person was never found. He wouldn't fail his Lilly; he'd find this Fuzz.

"Are you going to stand there all day, or you going to join your lovely lady?" Soaring Eagle stood, stretching. "I need to get some sleep. This old body can't do this late crap without lots of sleep, hence one of the reasons our meeting will be this afternoon."

"Right. You could outlast every one of us, old man," Dark Horse grumbled and pulled Soaring Eagle into a hug. "Thank you for being there."

"I'm not going anywhere. My wife made me promise to watch you, and I will. She always did have a soft spot for you." Soaring Eagle squeezed his shoulders before stepping back.

"I won't be here, but I'll know what is going on." Soaring Eagle gave him one of those looks that he used to give him as a child. and said, "After all I have eyes in the back of my head."

'Dark Horse shook his head. "You have a memory like a sponge, soaking up everything. Go get some sleep, and thank you for keeping Lilly company."

"It was my pleasure. She has a sharp mind and is beautiful. you are very lucky." Soaring Eagle closed the door behind him.

"I can see why you are drawn to that man. He is something special. There are few men left in this world like him and my father. It's sad, really, when you think about it," his Lilly said.

"I agree." He sat down with his plate of food then pointed at hers with his fork." How is everything?"

"You know it's awesome. Half of what I took is already gone. I knew you'd go for the steak. You seem like a beef and potatoes kind of guy." Lilly smiled, taking another bite of her ham.

"Do you want some?"

"No, but thank you. This ham is good and hits the spot. Soaring Eagle was telling me a bit about your culture. Do you really believe everything has a spirit?"

"Yes. Tell me, have you ever talked to your plants? Lifted your head to the cool breeze in the summer, just enjoying the scent as it caresses your skin?" He cut his steak then put a small portion of it on her plate. "Eat. I know you want a bite."

"Thank you." She smiled. "Yes, I've talked to my plants and never really thought of the wind, but you are right. Even last night on the back of your bike, it was as if the wind was washing away all the negativizes that clung to me."

"Yes, the wind does many things, spreads the seeds of plants, giving life, helps the flight of many animals and insects so they can survive. Sort of like you. You have different purposes also. You were put on this world to enhance it."

She snorted. "I don't know about that. I haven't done much."

"I disagree. Already, you have given me hope. Your father lives because of you, not to mention all the people you have helped in the ER. Earlier, you were talking about being worried about people of your town, a part of you. You are part of my circle of life, and I for one am very grateful to have you. I will remind you each and every day how important you are to me, little flower." He put down his fork and squeezed her hand. "Now, eat up. You need some sleep."

Lilly took a bite of food, glancing at the bed then at him. "Um, is the sofa a pullout?"

He smiled. "No, you will share my bed. But, not to worry. all I want to do is hold you. You are not ready for my loving yet, little flower." He met her gaze. "But soon."

Dark Horse noticed everything about his woman, when her nipples hardened, and her breathing increased. Oh, his little flower would be doing much more of that and soon, but not for the next few days. Until then, he would care for her. Helping to heal her soul, and right now, he was going to start. Stuffing a piece of steak into his mouth, Dark Horse got up and moved to the dresser where her gift was. He carefully picked up the box and returned to her side.

"I don't know why, but this was meant to be yours. I saw it in one of the windows when we stopped in a small town," he told her.

Tears filled her eyes, as she took the box, her hands shaking. Lilly pushed her dinner aside and set it on the table in front of her, running her fingers over the edge of it.

"It's stunning. My mom used to have a box like this. She kept everything my father had given her in it. Love letters, jewelry, and things like that. She and I would sit on her bed going through the box, and she'd tell me the stories for each item." Tears rolled down her cheeks as Lilly peered up at him. "Maybe I can do the same thing, if what you say is true?"

Dark Horse reached over and brushed the tears away. "I think that would be a wonderful idea. But I'm afraid I'm not much on love letters." He smiled.

She shrugged. "It will be our box." Lilly opened the box inhaling. "Cedar. God I love the smell of it. I used to have a hope chest made of cedar." Once more she peeked up at him. "I think I want to start a hope trunk. If what you say is going to happen."

"I'll make you one," Dark Horse offered, wanting to make her smile again.

"You can do that?"

He nodded. "When my mother was killed, I was angry, hated the world. Soaring Eagle plopped me down and gave me a chunk of wood and knife. 'Create something your mother would love,' he told me, and I did. It took a month, but I made my first wooden statue, a wooden lily."

Dark Horse moved to his personal belongings and took out the wrapped object. "My first gift for your box." He turned and handed her his lily."

Carefully, she unfolded the old wooden statue he carried around with him. She lifted the wooden flower up, her bottom lip started to shake, and her eyes watered again. "It's the most beautiful thing and our first story together," she whispered as she carefully wrapped it up again moving to the box, placing it in it. "If you'll excuse me, I need to take a shower."

Lilly had gone into the bathroom, when he remembered his

weapons were laid out on the counter. "Crap. Lilly, wait." He pushed open the bathroom door to see her staring at the knives. Thank god his gun was tucked away.

"These are all yours."

"Yes." He reached around the bathroom door and snatched up his bag to put his knives away.

"I didn't feel one of those on you." She almost appeared confused.

He smiled. "That is good. Most of them stay hidden, well, except this one." He picked up his special blade'. "This one you can't hide. I bought this the same place I found your box, our box. It has a special job to do, when I find him." Dark Horse growled and placed the knife in his bag. He lifted his, gaze meeting Lilly's.

"Don't ask. I promise I will always protect you and keep you from as much as I can, but I do have a dark side. I'm not an angel. You are my light through all of this. Only for you."

Lilly held up her hand. "Don't. We need to slow down." She started the shower.

"I thought you'd take a hot bath."

"No, not tonight." Keeping her back to him, she stripped out of her shirt. What he saw...

"Stop," he growled and stepped forward tracing the knife marks on her lower back.

"His mark. He did that the first time he raped me. Told me that any man who touched me would know I was his, even if he was dead," she whispered. "Do you think something like a tattoo would cover it?"

Dark Horse took two deep breaths. "Let me think of something." He ran his fingers over the initials in her skin, which was still a little pink. "I know it's too soon, but could you maybe think about wearing my mark here?" He held his breath, almost afraid the question would be too much.

His Lilly stripped the rest of the way and stepped into the shower. "We'll see, but I'd want to see what it is before it goes on my body and it's my body still." She shut the shower door.

He grinned. "We'll see, little flower. We'll see," Dark Horse mumbled then gathered the rest of his weapons, cleaning up the mess he had left in the bathroom and laying out clean towels.

Dark Horse tucked his knife under his pillow then put away the other knives before returning to finish his meal, thinking of a tattoo that would stand out on her back. He needed to talk with Night Wing, who could design anything. He'd already done the artwork on his horse and his chest piece.

A few minutes later, he rolled the food table outside in the hall, then locked up the room and turned to see Lilly standing there in the little T-shirt Kizzy had given her.

She looked like a flower with her pink toes, nipples hard, and her skin rosy from the hot water. Lilly smiled. "I hate to ask, but do you think you could help me with my hair. It's in knots and with no hair conditioner in there, well, it's a mess." She held up a brush and pointed to her long blonde hair.

He took her hand and pulled her to the bed. Sitting down on the bed, Dark Horse lifted Lilly and placed her between his legs, earning a squeak out of her.

"You could have hurt yourself. Don't do that." She glanced over her shoulder at him, giving him the brush.

"Please. You are too skinny as it is. Now, turn around and let's get these knots out. You need to sleep." For the next few minutes,

Dark Horse worked on Lilly's hair, careful of the stiches he encountered, and realized he loved to brush her hair.

"Your hair is so beautiful. I'll make sure to have conditioner brought up, too, but I'd like to do this every night. Would you allow me to help you?" He flinched, worried he'd sounded dorky.

Lilly glanced over her shoulder and smiled. "I'd love it. Having you brush my hair feels great. My mom used to do it before she died and then dad took over. With hair so fine, it's a chore to keep up, but I love it."

She took the brush out of his hand, placed a kiss on his cheek, and got off the bed. "Thank you." She placed the brush on the table and stared at the bed then at him.

He smiled and stood, turning the covers down. "Hop in, but be careful of my pillow," he warned her as he stripped out of his pants, waiting for her to settle down.

Her eyes grew large. "What are you doing?"

"I'm getting ready to sleep. Now, move it." He patted her butt.

"But you're naked," she squeaked.

***

Lilly didn't mind him being naked. It was the size of his cock that had her sputtering like a damn innocent, and she was from that. Not only was he thick, but he also had what was called a Prince Albert. Damn, she was in so much trouble.

Her gaze jumped to his smile. "What?" she squeaked.

Dark Horse leaned down until his nose bumped hers. "I love you staring at my body, but now is not a good time to test me little flower when we both know you are not ready yet." He nipped her

73

nose. "Now, get under the covers."

She scooted over, covering herself and burying her face in the other pillow, embarrassed by her own reaction.

But Dark Horse wasn't about to let her hide. Lying next to her, he wrapped his arms around her, pulling he back against him.

"Sleep, little flower, and know I'm here. You are safe," he told her, placing a kiss on the side of her neck.

He was big, and his body wrapped tightly around hers. Lilly had to admit she loved the cocoon feeling he was giving her, spooning her. He slid his hand up her stomach, resting it beneath her breast, his thumb stroking it. She took a deep, calming breath, He smelled of the soap she had used.

"Thank you, Dark Horse, for coming to help me."

"Hush, there is no need to thank me. Sleep, little one. We have a lot to do tomorrow."

Even with his thick hard cock against her ass, Lilly couldn't keep her eyes open. It was like her body knew she was safe for the first time in a while and was slowly shutting down. The last thing she heard was Dark Horse whispering to her that she was safe in his arms.

"Anyone who touches you will see my mark, property of the Irons," Fuzz said, as he used the flaming hot knife to cut into her skin. Her naked body was held by Fat Bob and two other men. Her screams woke her up. Sweat covered her face, and tears rolled down her cheeks, as Dark Horse came running into the room with two other men.

"Easy there, little flower." Dark Horse lifted her. "It was a nightmare nothing more." He held her tight, nodding to the two men who exited, giving her the time to get herself together.

Wiping away the tears and taking a deep breath, she peeked up at him. "What time is it?" Her voice cracked.

"It's still early, eleven. I had to talk with one of my men, but I did it out in the hall when I heard your scream. I have to say never since my mother's death have I been more scared."

"Sorry. I'm okay now." She scooted off his lap.

"Want to tell me about it?"

"Just reliving his markings. Guess I'll have dreams like that for a while." She noticed a pile of clothes on the dresser.

"Well, I'll just have to make sure I'm there to help you face those dreams," Dark Horse rose, pulling her into his arms. "The clothes are from Kizzy. She thinks they should fit. Don't ask me how she does it, but I'd wear the jeans since we'll be traveling back to your town to see what needs to be done."

"I did have a car. Do you think we could try and find it?" She went through the shirts, picking a nice large black cotton T-shirt.

"What kind of car? I can get word out to our men and have them keep an eye out for it."

She lifted the clothes up to her nose and smiled. "A Mustang, red." Lilly smiled up at him. "It's my first car. I made sure it was always cleaned and maintained."

"Mustang, nice. I'll make sure we find it and even if it's damaged, I can fix it. I've restored a number of old cars." He placed a kiss on the top of her head. "Go get dressed, little flower, it's time to get moving. I'll pack up the room. My men have found a place for us to stay at for the next year. We'll check it out this afternoon before your father gets out of hospital. I want to make sure we have everything he'll need."

Lilly glanced over her shoulder as she headed for the bathroom.

"Thank you. You don't know how much that means to me, knowing you are including my father."

"There is no need to thank me. What is important to you is important to me. I will always try and make sure you are happy, Lilly. There might be times we butt heads, but I will always listen. Your health and well-being are top priorities for me." He grabbed what appeared to be a new suitcase.

"Um, I hate to break it to you, but that isn't going to fit on your bike." She laughed.

He turned his dark eyes on her, smiling. "I know that, smarty pants. That's why we have a van and truck that carries our personal things and such."

Lilly nodded, remembering seeing them at her former house.. As soon as she peeked in the bathroom mirror, Lilly squeaked. "God I look like crap," she mumbled, putting her clothes on the counter and taking a washcloth to clean her face and wipe all sleep out of her eyes, hoping the cold water would ease some of the tenderness around her black eye and swollen cheek.

"You'll heal soon enough. If it was worse, I would have called Red Hawk, but I didn't want to drain him when he was helping heal some of your townspeople that were in serious condition."

"Is this Red Hawk a doctor?" She washed her face.

"No, it's more of a gift, but he knows all about herbs, and such. He was also a medic when his unit was shipped out. So, he has experience. Plus, Soaring Eagle is training him to take his place as the next medicine man."

Turning her head, Lilly cussed, getting soap in her eye. "Damn." She rinsed her face. "Go pack. You are distracting me," she grumbled then grabbed a towel to dry her face.

"It was your own fault, not paying attention to what you were doing. Pay attention." He leaned over and smacked her butt. "Get moving."

Lilly sighed. The man had an ass on him, that was for sure and he didn't wear baggy pants, thank god. She shook her head and turned to see him smiling at her.

"Not to worry, I love staring at your body, too."

"Smart ass." She shut the door on him, earning a laugh.

Lilly smiled, for the first time feeling a little ease in her chest, but there was still a threat out there until those four assholes were caught. Shaking her head, Lilly brushed her teeth and got dressed before searching for the brush to do her hair.

"I have the brush out here when you are ready," Dark Horse yelled.

She picked up her stuff and emerged into the room. "How did you know I was trying to find it?" She lifted her nightshirt.

He pointed to the open suitcase. "I just know. Now come and sit here. I told you I wanted to brush your hair, please." Dark Horse pulled the chair out from the table, waiting.

"You really like brushing my hair?" She sat at the table.

"Yes. As I told you, I used to do it for my mom. In the morning, and we'd talk about our day to come. She'd drink her coffee and ask me what happened the day before and what I intended to do to better myself that day." He took her hair into his hand and started to brush it.

"And what are we planning for today?" She noticed a mug of coffee sitting on the table. "For me?"

He nodded. "There is cream and sugar there, too. I didn't know how you like it." He stopped brushing her hair. "You do like it, right?"

"Try and take my coffee, you'll lose an arm," she grumbled and poured the cream into her coffee, taking a deep breath. "Love my coffee. I could drink this stuff all day. Hell, I could live in a coffee shop! Make note, my Dark Warrior, this flower will need coffee wherever we are," she mumbled before taking her first sip.

"Done. If there is a way I'll make sure you have your coffee. Maybe we should add that to the plants we will be growing. I'll have to ask around about that." Dark Horse nodded. "No sugar, just cream?"

She nodded. "I always wanted a greenhouse. where ever we are going to have this safe place, we should set that up right away. Also, you might want to talk with Cid. He lived outside of town so hopefully he wasn't affected by those assholes. But he loves animals. His chickens are the best, and so are his cows. He even bought a few buffalo. You might be able to come up with a way of saving his animals so we have them for the future."

"I'll do that, and I would like you to talk with Black Bull's wife. From what I understand, she's the canning queen. We'll need food supplies, and canning would be a help." Dark Horse laughed. "You need to speak with Kizzy. She'll have a notebook for you with all sorts of ideas. I believe when she shopped as we were coming here, she bought us things to use, too." He nodded to his cell phone. "She has all our numbers going to an answering machine. Her uncles have also picked up old-fashioned CB' radios and things we'll be setting up to keep in contact with the other safe places."

A small knock on their door had her turning her head to see Kizzy peeking inside. "Good, you're awake." Kizzy glanced behind her. "I told you she would be up," Kizzy mumbled, right before she jumped.

"Damn it, Running Wolf, stop it. Dark Horse is like a brother to you. Why shouldn't I consider him family?"

"You will always be my sister. Come on in. There is coffee over there on the dresser. I had a feeling you two would be here." Dark Horse took Lilly's coffee from her hands and stole a sip. Then he winked at her. "Thank you."

"You're lucky you are on my good side," she grumbled and took her coffee back, earning a snort from Running Wolf as he came in carrying their little girl.

"How did you sleep?" He sat down as Kizzy poured coffee.

"She had a nightmare this morning, but other than that she slept like a log. You should hear her little snores." Dark Horse grinned from ear to ear.

"What? I don't snore." She glared up at him.

"Yes, you do, but not to worry. They were cute little things, not like Red Hawk."

Running Horse laughed.

Chapter Seven

The Earth laughs in flowers.
Ralph Waldo Emerson

Lilly inched closer to Dark Horse as they stepped into the conference room where over three hundred men were eating and waiting for them to come down.

Soaring Eagle, Black Bull, Raining Song, and Seeking Elk sat at a head table with what appeared to be their wives.

Yes, this massive group was impressive and could be scary to a small-town woman like his Lilly. Dark Horse tightened his hold as Running Wolf and Kizzy approached.

"Damn, impressive," Kizzy whispered.

"Nice turnout. Almost as big as one of our family reunions," Stephan replied from behind them.

Kizzy peeked over her shoulder. "What are you talking about? We never had a family reunion this big."

"Oh, sweet Kizzy, you've only been to the smaller ones. There is one in Europe that is massive. The last time I went to it was the year before your father died. There had to be close to six hundred of us."

Kizzy screeched and ran to one of her family members, hugging her, then the three children with her. Behind them was Santana. "I don't understand, I thought all the children were going to Canada."

"Santana is staying here with Dark Horse." Stephan glanced at his brother. "It seems someone here has interested our Santana, enough to bring his children."

"Who?" Kizzy asked.

"That is for me to know, so stay out of it, Kizzy. Plus, there are a few members of our distant family around this area. I'll be meeting with them and bringing them here when the time is right. Plus, I do believe Dark Horse may need a steadier head around to help him."

Stephan laughed. "Right. You have a temper twice that of mine. I warn you both." Stephan glared at Santana then at him. "If anything happens to you two, I'll personally come back down here and kick some serious butt. Understand me?" he growled, earning some giggles from the little girls and a laugh from the little boy.

Santana shook his head. "Welcome to the family, Dark Horse, and get used to Stephan butting into your business."

"I hate to break this up, but we need to go in. They're waiting for us," Running Wolf told them, turning to Dark Horse. "You ready to take the lead?"

"As ready as anyone is." He glanced down at Lilly rubbing her arm. "We'll do this together," he told her and she nodded.

"I'm not ready to speak with all these people, Dark Horse," she whispered.

"Not to worry. You just eat and write down questions that pop up in your head as we talk." Dark Horse smiled. "You have the notebook and pen Kizzy gave you."

Kizzy smacked his arm. "Hey, you want us to keep organized. This is way too important not to be."

Lilly laughed. "I have to agree with Kizzy. Organization, and plans are important if we are going to set this up. I'll take notes and show Dad. He'll have some great points to make, too, since he knows how to build those underground things."

"You know I'll listen to him. After all, he kept you alive till I could get to you." He kissed the top of her head.

"Yeah, alive," she mumbled. All eyes turned to them as they made their way to the front table. He knew his Lilly was thinking about the beatings and things when she shivered next to him.

He leaned down as he pulled out her chair, whispering into her ear. "He didn't touch your soul little flower, that is all mine. But soon enough I will erase all of those nightmares, I promise." He kissed her cheek as she sat down.

She reached up and patted his arm. "You already eased some of the tensions. Thank you." She took out her notebook and pen, as Kizzy did the same next to her.

"Don't say a word." Lilly winked at him, and he grinned, taking his seat next to her as food was brought out to them, along with juice, coffee, and water.

For the next hour, Soaring Eagle and Black Bull answered questions, then two of Running Wolf's men rose. Two Eyes and Raining Tom. "We will be staying here, since our families are close. My uncle has an ancient map of the area that might help find this place we are to be at."

Soaring Eagle nodded. "Go to your uncle's and bring the map to Dark Horse tonight. We'll have fire. Maybe our Kizzy would dance for us again?" Soaring Eagle grinned, as Running Wolf growled.

Kizzy laughed. "I'd love to dance. Maybe I'll teach Lilly some dance moves before we leave."

A low rumble rang in his ears, and not until Lilly placed her hand on his arm, r smiling at him did he realize it was him growling.

"Not to worry. I have two left feet," she teased, earning laughs all around.

"Oh, you don't have to move your feet to much, just your hips and other body parts" Kizzy wiggled her eyebrows. "And your body parts are perfect for dancing."

Running Wolf groaned. "I'm so sorry, Dark Horse. I should have brought her ball gag down with us." He spoke loud enough for everyone to hear.

Kizzy's face turned pink, and she sputtered. "You wouldn't dare! Not if you want to touch me!"

"Children, we are getting off the subject here," Soaring Eagle said, coming over to Kizzy and Running Wolf, squeezing both of their shoulders. "Lilly, we're going to count on you to help with this area. What is the biggest town close to your little city where you would trust authorities?"

"Your best bet would be to go to Daingerfield for anything big you need. I go there to do most of our big time shopping for the house." Lilly reached under the table, grabbing onto his leg. "I really hate being the center of attraction," she whispered to him, leaning over.

At once, Dark Horse pulled her chair closer to his and laid his arm over the back of her chair. He leaned over and placed a kiss on the side of her neck. "Everyone here would protect you with their life little flower. Never be afraid of my people, because now they are yours."

"We aren't married yet," she whispered back. "I don't even know you, any of you."

Kizzy must have felt her nervousness, because she reached over and squeezed her arm. "They really are harmless, well, unless you go against them or attack one of theirs. You're part of this family now even though you are not married. Now, eat. There is a lot of work to do, and you don't want to be sick when you pick up your father."

Dark Horse shook his head as both of them dug into their food.

Between bites, Lilly peeked over at him, then she'd scan the room, watching little things as they talked among themselves. "You know I never heard of these tunnels. Are you sure they are here, Dar Horse?".

"They are there child. Just no one has found them, but we will."

She nodded. "Wow, he has some hearing."

Soaring Eagle laughed and Dark Horse grinned. "When you are trained like the old days, you learn to listen, see your surroundings. For example, the waitress." He pointed with this knife. "She has a tattoo on her lower arm and one on her leg. Little things normal people wouldn't see, we were taught at a young age to search for. Maybe its best we were taught that way. Ever since the white man came over, we have been fighting for our rights."

Lilly lifted her knife up and pointed to Black Bull as he walked by. "Like the fact that your friend there needs to have his thyroid checked."

"What? What are you talking about?"

"Dark Horse you are not the only one who can spot things. The lump at his throat." She took another bite as he called Red Hawk over to their table.

"Please, tell him what you told me," Dark Horse said.

"Is he a doctor? It will take a doctor to do the testing and stuff if I'm right. Cancer is not something you want to mess with." Lilly stuffed another piece of sausage in her mouth.

"Who?" Red Hawk scanned around the room at the group of his warriors.

Lilly waved her fork then took a drink and set it down. "Black Bull."

85

"I haven't been introduced to him." Red Hawk frowned, as Soaring Eagle came over, not looking too happy.

"What's all the commotion? I heard Black Bull's name, and it's rude to talk about someone when he's here." Soaring Eagle said.

"Lilly believes Black Bull is sick with cancer." Dark Horse didn't like Soaring Eagle's comment.

A loud whistle sounded next to him. Lilly jumped and grabbed her chest. "Warn me when you do that." She gulped down the food in her mouth.

"I just got her calm," Kizzy grumbled.

"Sorry daughter." Soaring Eagle pointed at Black Bull. "Come here, please."

"Nothing like being put on the spot," Lilly groaned.

"This is important. You're an ER nurse. I take your word on this." Dark Horse told her.

Red Hawk studied the warrior. He was older than Dark Horse, and he could see the battle scars, emotionally and physically on him.

"What can I help you with?" Black Bull gave Soaring Eagle a puzzled look, which only made his mentor laugh.

"This young lady is worried about your health. She says you should seek a doctor for that lump on your throat." Soaring Eagle pointed to the small lump.

***

Lilly didn't say anything as this Red Hawk stepped closer, staring at the worrisome lump. They would either believe her or they wouldn't.

But Lilly sure hoped Dark Horse did.

Dark Horse had a strong chin, high cheekbones, and a small scar on under his left eye, that had her reaching up, but then she stopped pulling her hand back.

Dark Horse turned his eyes on her and winked, squeezing her knee under the table.

"I have a feeling your Lilly might be right on this. Would you allow me, Black Bull?" Red Hawk asked.

"Have you dealt with this before?" Running Wolf asked.

"No, but I can try." Red Hawk glanced at Lilly. "What is the normal treatment for something like this?"

Lilly reached for Dark Horse's hand, twining his fingers with hers. "It all depends on how far the cancer has spread. First and second stages, usually partial or total removal of the thyroid and treatment. But I'm not a doctor. He needs one who specializes in this. I can recommend someone good at the hospital, Mr. Black Bull."

"Even if I can do something, I would suggest you take Ms. Lilly up on her offer to make sure that I have gotten all the cancer if it is what she says," Red Hawk cautioned.

Black Bull glanced back at the table where his wife sat. He held out his hand, and she came to him. "Why don't you get the information from Lilly while I go with Red Hawk. While I'm doing this you, Lilly, and Kizzy can start planning." He leaned down and placed a kiss on her cheek.

Dark Horse stood. "Do not worry about your wife. She will be safe with us. Go with Red Hawk and see what he can do. Maybe the Great Mother will help us one more time."

Lilly stood, gathering another chair, and motioned for the waitress, asking her to bring Black Bull's wife's plate over.

"I thank you both. We are in your debt." Black Bull followed Red Hawk out of the diner.

Soaring Eagle guided the tall, full-figured woman over to them. "Lilly, Kissy, this is Kia Black Bull. If you ladies will excuse us, we'll make sure Red Hawk and Black Bull are taken care of."

"Please sit." Lilly smiled up at Dark Horse as he placed a kiss on the top of her head.

"You okay?"

She scanned around her and nodded. "I'll write down the name of the best doctor and give it to Kia." Lilly frowned, leaning over to see Kizzy. "You know, we might want to list plants that fight cancer. I know there are a few herbs that help."

Kizzy flipped through one of her notebook. "I have mint, parsley, thyme, sage, rosemary, and oregano, so far. What else do you suggest we start growing."

"I have basil, cilantro, and aloe vera growing right now, along with a few of what Kizzy has listed off," Kia replied.

"All of those are good, but we should also gather nasturtium, ginger, turmeric, also small tomatoes." Lilly tapped her fingers. "I think I'll have to contact Dr. Fox. he's the best herbal doctor around. He'll be able to help us, and I think Red Hawk would have a list we can compare it to." Lilly took a sip of coffee, watching those around her come and go, but noticed that two men at each end of the table, standing and watching.

"Our guards," Kizzy whispered as a waitress placed a covered dish in front of Lilly.

Frowning, she stared up at the woman to ask her what it was, but she was already gone. "Weird." Lilly reached for the cover as Kizzy grabbed her hand and yanked her away.

"No, get back both of you," she hissed as her uncle Stephan rushed over.

"What?" He glanced at Kizzy as Lilly scooted away from the table at the same time Kia did.

"Harvestman," Kia whispered.

"What is harvestman?" Lilly asked as Dark Horse, Running Wolf, and Black Bull stormed into room and right to their sides.

Dark Horse checked her from head to toe, before framing her face with his hands. "You okay?"

"I'm fine. Just trying to figure out what is going on."

Soaring Eagle reached over to her plate cover.

Three large live scorpions scattered around the table. "They're here," she whispered, a chill going up her back. "He's not going to let go, no matter what." Lilly shook, grabbing onto Dark Horse's arm. "Your friends could have been killed." She stepped away from him, but Dark Horse growled, yanking her back into his arms, hugging her tight.

"Don't think it. You are going nowhere without me," he growled. "Find that waitress now, and I want to know how they got inside."

"Dark Horse your friends could have been harmed. Maybe I should go somewhere away from everyone," Lilly tried to tell him, but he wasn't hearing any of it.

"No." He held her at his side as men took off and the scorpions were killed.

Lilly was getting pissed as he talked with his warriors, holding onto her. "Damn it, Dark Horse, let go. I want to make sure Kia and Kizzy are okay."

Dark Horse glanced around before nodding. "Do not go anywhere else."

She rolled her eyes and made her way over to the girls as another chair was placed near the ladies.

"I thought he would never let you go." Kizzy smiled and reached over, squeezing her hand.

"I kind of suggested he let me leave. Needless to say, he's not very happy," Lilly mumbled.

"It's this whole situation. Thank god we have houses to go to today. Running Wolf and I will be staying for the next week to help find the tunnels and get you set up. We also need to find those assholes. You guys can't get organized if you have to keep checking over your shoulder," Kizzy growled.

Lilly nodded. "I'm kind of worried about my father being in the open hospital. I know Dark Horse has men there, but we were surrounded by men and they still managed to get close." She frowned then turned to Kia. "I'm sorry. Did Red Hawk have time to see if he could help?"

"That is why he isn't here. Even though he cautioned us and told us to see your specialist, which we agreed to do. With everything going on we need to make sure. What are we going to do about all the medical advances we have accomplished?" Kia rubbed her belly.

Lilly placed her hand over Kia's. "How far along are you?"

Kia smiled. "Three months. What do we do about vaccine's. There are so many questions and so little time. I know there are mothers who haven't gotten their children vaccinated, but with everything going on with the changes in the Earth, it has me worried."

Lilly patted her arm frowning. "You are right, but you have to remember to a lot of your protections will be passed onto your child. I think the first thing we should do is think of what medical aspects are we going to have. Kizzy, Red Hawk will be going with you?"

Kizzy nodded, frowning. "We also have a doctor meeting us in Canada. Maybe you can get a few of your doctors to help out, too. Do you think they would believe what is happening, or would they well just say we're all nuts?"

"Well we have the herbalist, and I know he for sure will help us, even Dr. Strebow the cancer doctor I suggested for Black Bull. Nice man, and his wife works right beside him, doing research. Oh my god." Lilly turned, smiling at both Kizzy and Kia. "The CEO, Doctor Rein of the hospital is a doomsday prepper. He is going to be a big help. Damn, I need my notebook and pen." Lilly looked around and noticed it at the table she had left. "Hold on. Let me go grab mine so I can write this all down." Lilly got up and headed toward the table when she was grabbed around the waist.

Natural instinct kicked in, and Lilly whirled around, going to shove her hand into the person's nose when she saw it was Dark Horse. Her heart in her throat, and breath gone, she glared at the gorgeous man. "*Don't do that*," she ground out bending down, trying to get her heart back to normal and her breathing.

"I'm sorry, little flower." Dark Horse bent down, staring into her eyes.

She blew out a breath and straightened up. "It's okay. I guess it's going to take time. Now, did you want something?" Lilly turned to move again toward the table and her notebook.

"I was wondering where you were going?" He smiled, seeing her picking up her notebook and pen.

"I remembered some people who might help us with the medical aspect of this new journey we are planning and wanted to write them down," she rambled on. "Do you think my father is okay?"

Dark Horse pulled out his phone. "Call the hospital and check on him. But rest assured I heard from both of the guards, and they are on alert. We have about thirty minutes before we leave. Everything is packed in the van, so we know they didn't get hold of anything. I'm afraid we lost one man. That's how they were able to get in here." He turned his gaze to the corner of the room.

"Oh my god. I need to speak with her please. This is my fault I need to apologize." Tears filled her eyes as she moved toward the woman.

"You are not at fault. Here they are," Dark Horse growled, wrapping his arm around her waist, moving with her.

"Your men wouldn't be in danger if not for me, and you know it," Lilly replied.

The woman moved out of another woman's arms. "You are not at fault Lilly. My man was one of the best, these assholes will pay for what they have done to you and Tex. I'm called Sunflower." The woman hugged her tight.

Lilly hugged her back, crying with her. "I'm so sorry, Sunflower. I just wish this nightmare would end. So many have been hurt and killed." Lilly stepped back into Dark Horse's arms. "If you need anything, please don't hesitate to ask. I know most of the people around here."

"Thank you. I'd like to stay and help out with the planning it is what Tex would want," Sunflower announced.

"We would be honored to have you here helping us. Please, allow Soaring Eagle to prepare Tex and Sunflower, take it slow."

Sunflower smiled. "Tex told you?" She placed her hand on her belly. "It's the only thing that is keeping me going, knowing I have a part of him growing inside of me."

"Congrats, I know Kia is expecting, too. This is exciting, two little ones to help us remember we are fighting for their world. It will give others hope when things get low. So, in some ways, your Tex is still helping," Lilly told her.

Soaring Eagle came over and wrapped his arm around Sunflower. "Come, let me take you to the car, and we can discuss what needs to be done." The older man glanced at Lilly. "You are indeed perfect for our Dark Horse. Everyone is ready to leave."

Lilly glanced back over her shoulder, sure only they and a few of Dark Horse's men. Even Kizzy and Kia were gone.

She shook her head and muttered, "So out of my league."

Chapter Eight

"She is like a fawn, watching, learning as his Lilly takes the first steps to healing her soul."
Dark Horse

Dark Horse kept a close eye on Lilly as they moved through the rental house his men had found them. It was a four-bedroom home, on three acres of land just outside her home town and easy to defend.

Right now, ten of his men were setting up perimeter traps, cameras, and such. Dark Horse was not going to be caught with his guard down again.

"I think your father would like this room. It has its own bathroom and is on the bottom floor, so no stairs," Dark Horse told her, breaking the silence. "You don't mind if Running Wolf and Kizzy stay with us since they will only be here a few days?" he asked as Stephan pulled their trailer in the back, followed by Running Wolf."

He reached out and pulled Lilly into his arms, hugging her tight while resting his head on hers. "What's wrong?"

"I guess I'm just trying to absorb everything. Do you know how dangerous it's going to be after people start figuring out things are really going downhill? There's going to be fighting." She shivered. "And other things."

Dark Hunter wound his hand in her hair, and pulled her head back, staring into her face. The doubt and fear ate at his heart and gut. "My little flower, it will be dangerous. I'm not going to lie. It's one of the reasons why you must listen to me. I will do everything to protect you and your father," he told her, covering her mouth with his.

She tasted of coffee as Dark Horse slid his tongue inside, loving her tongue as he planned to do to her body. The first time he had seen her in the shelter peeking up at him, with tears in her eyes, he'd known he was lost.

He lifted his head, nipping her bottom lip. "Is this place okay?"

"It's fine, and you shouldn't have done that?" Lilly stepped back as he gave her room, knowing Running Wolf and Kizzy were coming up to the house.

"I plan and doing that all the time, my little flower. You need to get used to my touch. Slowly, I'll wipe out those nightmares." He cupped her cheek. "And replace them with memories that will not only make you blush when you think of them, but your need for my dark loving—"

Lilly covered his mouth with her hand and he nipped it. "They're here, hush."

"Don't worry about them. Believe me, Running Wolf has already given his woman such memories," he growled, swatting her butt then turning to greet his friend.

"We have a surprise for you, Lilly." Running Wolf stepped aside as Stephan helped her father into the room.

"Daddy," Lilly whispered, going to him and wrapping her arms around him, crying.

"It's okay little flower. Your Dr. Morree gave me the all clear, but it didn't hurt that your man's friend Red Hawk paid me a visit. I swear that man is a miracle worker. I feel twenty years younger."

"I remember this place. It was old man Jeb's farm. Him and his wife ran the place till his kids came and took them to Florida with them. If I'm not mistaken it's a little bigger than our place was." Her father started to walk out of the bedroom into the living room. "Did they leave all the furniture, Dark Horse?"

"Yes, all the furniture came with it. We've ordered a few more beds, though, which should be arriving this afternoon for the upstairs and your room down here. I believe Santana ran to the grocery store for us?"

Stephan nodded. "Yes, he and Mason both went we'll have a well-stocked kitchen in a few hours."

Kizzy groaned. "You should have let one of us go with them." She shook her head. "Well, we can pick up what they don't get when I take Lilly to get some clothes and things tomorrow."

"Excuse me? I didn't hear you right." Running Wolf growled, holding their daughter in one hand and reaching out grabbing a handful of Kizzy's hair and pull her head back.

"Maybe I need to cut my hair," Lilly grumbled, frowning at him, wondering if he'd do the same thing.

"You will not," her father yelled at the same time Dark Horse did.

"Jeez." Lilly rolled her eyes. "But Kizzy is right. I need to go the store. Dad doesn't have many clothes, and neither do I. Can I use your phone?" she asked Dark Horse. "I want to call my bank see what is going on with my accounts." Lilly glanced at her father. "Did you call?"

He nodded. "The savings is intact, but I'm afraid they wiped anything I had in the checking. I'm lucky I kept the majority of my money in a separate account."

Lilly nodded to her father, dialing her bank as he sat down at the kitchen table with her. By the time she got off the phone, Lilly was furious.

They had wiped out her checking account, over two thousand gone, but her savings hadn't been touched. Just like her father she too had put her savings into another account. Her cards were maxed to the limit, but two of the companies were taking care of it for her.

"Well?" Dark Horse placed the phone back in his pocket.

"My checking account wiped out and two cards at the max, but the banks are taking care of that. I will need to run to the bank. They are going to have a card waiting for me and a new checking account," Lilly tapped her fingers on the table.

Dark Horse put his hands on her shoulders and squeezed. "We have your belonging from the shelter to go through and new beds coming today. Can you wait and we'll take you tomorrow? I'd really like to get our defenses up and get settled in here first before we go out."

"Makes sense." Her father nodded. "I already have the meds. Dr. Morree had the hospital fill them before I left for me. If they are bringing food and beds, I say we can last till tomorrow. Plus, Lilly, there enough clothes of yours to last you a few days. You'd know if you would have gone through the boxes while stuck in the shelter."

Lilly snorted. "When? When I was watching Fuzz trying to get across the ravine so he could find me, I couldn't concentrate on much. Sorry, Daddy." Lilly reached over and squeezed his arm. "A few days won't matter right now. Hell, I don't know if I'm ready to face the world right now anyway." She took a deep breath. "Okay, where are our belongings? I can start going through them."

"We're bringing them in now. Let Kizzy help you while we start getting the security system up along with our defense system outside." Running Wolf handed their little girl to his wife.

"Do we have a washer and dryer here? We really need to wash some clothes, and I have a feeling a lot of their clothes are going to smell like smoke." Kizzy shook her head.

"That is true, but we're going to need laundry detergent," Lilly said.

"Got it." Kizzy's uncle Santana carried in bags of groceries.

"And yes, there is a washer and dryer made sure of it before we purchased the house." Stephan brought in more bags as others started to bring in their belongings from the hideout her father had built.

Kizzy reached over and squeezed her arm. "You start going through your belongings while I put away the food and stuff. You can move things around later if you don't like where I put it." She smiled. "It will keep us both busy, and when we're done with this, we can sit down and go over how we are to start this amazing thing of saving all these people."

"Now, that statement is right. There is nightmare, but agreed. I have a feeling you are going to get done way before I am," Lilly moaned, seeing the pile in the living room getting bigger and bigger.

"I can help, too." Her father stood.

"Nope, You are going to get sit on your butt in that comfy chair there and relax, Dad. You' had stints put in just the other day. We will do this slowly, because I so don't need you away from me right now." Lilly turned her gaze on him. "Please."

Her father grumbled all the way to the chair. "I do this under protest, and the fact that I can't stand seeing your tears."

Duly noted and you," Lilly turned to Dark Horse, leaning

99

against the wall watching her. "I know you have things you want to do so scat. Let us handle this for now and I promise not to leave the house today."

Dark Horse moved like a mountain lion, stalking toward her with grace and purpose. He wrapped his arms around her and yanked her into his body. He wrapped his hand around her braid and pulled her head back to stare down at her.

"You're getting a little bossy there, my little flower." He nipped her nose. "I can actually see you at work in the ER. You will handle this fine, but remember I am here to help. Call on me, Lilly flower and don't be lifting anything too heavy today. You've been through enough. Allow some of our men to help if you want anything moved. We'll be right outside if you need us," he told her then covered her mouth in what she thought would be a hard, punishing kiss but wasn't. Dark Horse kissed her as if she was something precious, fragile.

Dark Horse lifted his head, stepping back with a cocky grin on his face. "Behave, little flower, and don't do too much." With that, he walked out outside, and Lilly swore the air crackled around him, full of energy.

"Well, shit," she mumbled, glancing over her shoulder to see her father smiling from ear to ear.

Kizzy handed her a laundry basket. "Afraid they are all like that. Every single damn biker," she grumbled. "One minute they are growling, the next they turn their attention on you. It's like being doused with boiling water. And it only gets stronger as your bond grows." She nodded to the basket. "Figured you could put the clothes that smell like fire in here, and we can start laundry while we work."

"You go ahead and start your load. It's going to take me some time to sort through this. We have plenty of time to do laundry," Lilly moaned the last part. "You do realize we are going to have to wash our clothes by hand?" She sat next to the growing pile of their belongings.

For the next two hours, Lilly went through ten boxes, putting things away, sorting through clothes while talking with Kizzy.

Already, they had a list of things that would have to be ordered. Lilly grabbed her laptop and sat down in the kitchen while her father took a nap in the chair.

Kizzy handed her a pop then sat next to her. "We have subs in the fridge for when the men come in for lunch." She picked up the list. "Sometimes, when I skim over my notes, it scares the crap out of me. Dark Horse is right, Lilly. With all the changes coming, we need to start really leaning on them more. Don't get me wrong. We can do a lot, but they were taught the old ways, how to survive. We weren't."

"It just seems like things are moving so fast, that I'm spinning around and I can't catch up with anything. Then there is this thing with Dark Horse. I mean, I just met the man last night, but inside it feels like I've been waiting my whole life for him." She shook her head then tapped the button to start her computer.

"Believe me, I know what you are going through. In a matter of days, I met and wed Running Wolf, not to mention almost dying, too." Kizzy shivered. "Well, I actually did die a few times before Red Hawk could save me.

Lilly reached over and squeezed her hand. "Believe me, been there, and I hope not to go through that again for a long time. Fuck." She stared at the video of Fuzz raping her.

Lilly didn't move and didn't know how long she sat there till strong arms lifted her and held her close. "Easy there, Lilly Flower. I've got you," Dark Horse whispered. He carried her into the living room, sitting down on one of the couches just holding her, rubbing her back, giving her the time to slowly come back to her surroundings.

Lilly buried her face into Dark Horse's shirt, holding on tight to it. "He's not going to give up on me," she finally got out, looking up at him. "I feel so dirty, like he was just here again."

"Well you're not dirty. You smell of lavender, and I know for a fact the bastard hasn't been here. I won't allow him to hurt you again, Lilly." Dark Horse hugged her tight.

"But he has my new email." She frowned and lifted her head, peering into the kitchen where Stephan sat at her computer, embarrassed he was seeing what they had done to her. She stared down at her hands. "Do you think he can find out where we are through my laptop?"

"Lilly, he's bound to find us. There are too many of our men moving around for them not to. But we want him to find us, because they are going to make a move and that is when we end this once and for all." Dark Horse kissed the top of her head when she stiffened and turned to him.

"You want him to find us, me?" Lilly squeaked and shook her head at him. "I can't see him again, Dark Horse." She rubbed her hands up awn on her pants. "I'm not that strong,"

"Oh, Lilly, you are stronger than you believe, but not to worry you won't see him again if I can help it. No, this time he will deal with me and only me," Dark Horse wrapped his arms tighter round her and pulled her back against him... "You okay?"

"I will be." She took a deep breath. "Thank you."

"Don't thank me for this, little flower. I will always be here for you."

Chapter Nine

He is richest who is content with the least, for content is the wealth of nature.

Socrates

Dark Horse set Lilly at the kitchen table and placed a sub and drink in front of her. "Eat." He pointed then grabbed another sandwich from Running Wolf.

"He's going to make his move soon. He's furious we have won and won't stop now." Running Wolf drew Lilly's attention.

"It's what we want, now stop worrying," Dark Horse told her. "Eat and tell us what is on that list of yours so far." He leaned down inches from her face. "Oh, and don't think we aren't going to have a little chat about you moving those boxes when I made sure you understood to call for help."

Lilly reached over, placing her small hand on his face, and pushing him back. "The boxes were nothing compared to moving an unconscious body, jeez," she said and froze.

Dark Horse his head back and laughed. "You are precious, my little flower, but I meant what I told you. I don't care if you can lift boxes. You've been through enough lately, and I want you to be able to recoup for a few days. Now, finish eating and we'll take that ride into town, but you will listen to every word I say, Lilly, when it comes to your safety." He stared at her, waiting for her to agree.

"Believe me, I'm going to be your shadow for a few days. The thought of running into..." Lilly's body shook, and she took a deep breath.

"If I had it my way, you wouldn't have to see them at all." He sighed.

"We all wish you and your friends wouldn't have to deal with them, but we just couldn't get the bastard. Of course, they wouldn't fight like real warriors," Running Wolf grumbled.

Kizzy snorted. "When have you ever run across an ass like them who would? Men like this Fuzz and the sheriff don't care about anyone but themselves, and believe me, there are a lot more men like him around." Kizzy took a bite of her sandwich.

"I have a feeling that is why your Great Mother is doing this now. We have destroyed so much, mankind has gotten lazy and greedy." Lilly's father came to stand behind his daughter. "You will promise me you will listen to Dark Horse, Lilly."

Lilly peered over her shoulder and smiled up at her father. "I promise, Daddy." she patted his hand on her shoulder. "Now, go finish your food and keep Soaring Eagle company. I set up the chess board. Does Soaring Eagle know how to play?"

Dark Horse laughed. "Watch him, I swear he uses his gift to help him win all the time," He gave Soaring Eagle a wide berth as he passed.

"You just don't pay attention, and I'd love to play a game with you. I'm afraid my warriors haven't given me any challenge lately." He returned to the living room.

"Hey now, I almost beat you last night," Jay Bird informed them, coming inside.

"Almost does not count in the game of chess." Soaring Eagle sighed, sitting down on the couch across from Lilly's father. "The younger generation."

Lilly's father laughed. "I expect my daughter back here with not a scratch on her." He held his gaze. "And if she does not listen, spank her ass." He arched an eyebrow at her.

"Hey now," she managed around a bite of food.

"I mean what I said, Lilly. Your man has my permission to spank you if you don't listen." Her father smiled. "I'll never forget the time your mother...well, needless to say your mother found my hand on her ass a number of times."

"And did she get to spank you when you did somethings stupid, too?" She faced him. "Because I know there have been a few times someone should have—"

"Watch it, little girl," her father interrupted her, turning his full attention on her.

"I swear this room is filled with too much testosterone, how about you all beat on your chests not on our asses." she grumbled, causing Kizzy to spit out her food laughing.

Dark Horse reached over and tugged on her hair. "We have enough to do, little flower." He smiled and placed a kiss on the top of her head. "Jay Bird, round the men up. We're going to town and make sure they are ready for anything. We'll be ready in ten minutes."

"I want to see you pound your chest." Kizzy smiled.

"Keep it up and you'll feel me spanking your butt," Running Wolf growled. "And, Kizzy, you will listen to me, or so help me, I'll send you to Canada with your uncles."

Kizzy waved her hand. "I always listen to you." She earned a moan from Stephan and Running Wolf. "And take into consideration what you tell me. But if something needs to be done I can't..." Kizzy didn't say anything else as Running Wolf moved and swept her up into his arms, over his shoulder where he slapped her butt hard.

"That's where your problem lies. You don't take in consideration that we have asked you to do something that would keep you safe. We'll meet you outside while I have serious talk with my wife." Running Wolf left of the kitchen, heading toward the room they were staying in.

"Don't you think that was a bit much? She wasn't doing anything wrong." Lilly frowned and put her napkin on the table, turning to see where Running Wolf had gone with Kizzy.

Kneeling in front of Lilly, Dark Horse turned her chair around to face him. "Running Wolf and I can't emphasize how important it is that you two start to listen to us. On every aspect, Lilly. We're not going to be gentle. You need to learn this right away. Our world is changing as we sit here." Dark Horse blew out his breath and reached up, cupping her cheek.

"Hell, we don't even know if new life forms will emerge, or old ones will die. We can't take one thing for granted." He stood, turning toward where Soaring Eagle sat with her father. They both nodded.

"This new world is going to be exciting and scary for all of us. I need you at my side, Lilly, and if that means spanking your cute butt because you didn't listen, putting yourself in danger I have no problem in doing it. Go get the coat I got for you, it's time to go."

"Lilly stood going toward the living room but stopped and turned to peer over her shoulder at him. "But what about you? If you do something I thought you shouldn't do, I get to spank you? I mean you do have a nice little—" Lilly screamed and ran as he lunged for her.

"No one spanks me, my little flower," he growled, following her into their room and shutting the door, trapping them in there.

Chapter Ten

Nature is the source of all true knowledge. She has her own logic, her own laws, she has no effect without cause nor invention without necessity.

Leonardo Da Vinci

Lilly spun around while backing up, staring at the man who had saved her life and many others. The heat in his eyes had her shaking her head. "I was kidding," she squeaked and fell onto the bed, but before Lilly could move, he was covering her body with his muscular one, staring down at her.

"This is no joke Lilly. I need to make sure you understand how dangerous it's going to get. People are going to be flipping out, hurting others, and such. Not to mention, we don't know how far the Great Mother is going to take things." He leaned down, bit her bottom lip, and pulled on it.

"How long do you think we'll have to be below?" she asked when he released her lip, her hands now twined with his above her head.

"I don't know, Lilly, but we'll survive if you listen to everything I tell you." He jumped off her and pulled her up as the roar of bikes could be heard coming down the street. "Get your coat. They're here."

"Do you really believe...he'll try and make a move in town?" A little tremor went through Lilly as he helped her with her coat.

"I'm counting on it and Lilly, if I capture him, you will ride back

with Mason, Kizzy's brother in the van. I'll be back later tonight."
Dark Horse moved toward the door.

"Wait, what are you going to do?" Lilly placed her hand onto his arm, stopping him from leaving.

"You don't need to know. But after tonight I can promise you the four of them will be gone from this world," He wrapped his arm around her, his hand resting on her butt cheek as he escorted her out to his bike.

Lifting his coat off his bike, Lilly could see the many weapons hidden in it, but she also knew he carried a few close to his skin, too.

"I was thinking maybe you should show me how to throw a knife. I don't want a gun, but I should know how to use a knife, especially if we are going to be cooking game." Lilly climbed on the back of the bike and wrapped her arms around Dark Horse.

"When things settle down we'll find you a nice hunting knife, but, Lilly, I will make sure you will never have to use it for self-defense. I'm sorry, but you will have to be protected, and if that means assigning ten men to you, so be it," he informed her then started up his bike.

"That is silly. Why tie up so many men? All you have to do is teach me a few tricks, how to use a knife, and I'll be able to take care of myself." She placed her helmet over her head, but Dark Horse was silent and pulled the bike out on the road.

"You can ignore me all you want, but if I have to take a class, I will. I'd prefer you to teach me, but I won't feel helpless again, Dark Horse. I mean it."

Dark Horse ignored her until they stopped at a light and Running Wolf pulled up next to them with Kizzy behind him.

Lilly would bet a hundred dollars her new friend was wishing she could clobber Running Wolf with a frying pan in the head by the glare she was giving him.

Kizzy turned her gaze to her and nodded.

"We have two following us," Running Wolf informed them, opening the microphone so they could hear him. "My guess is the other two are already in the town waiting."

"I was hoping this would happen. Is the sheriff's office still protected?" Dark Horse turned toward Running Wolf.

"Yes, we can leave the ladies there as soon as they make their move. Mason and Jay Bird both know to take them there the first sign of trouble."

Everyone remained quiet as they pulled into the small town. Some houses were gone, torched, while others had boarded-up windows. But what had Lilly shaking her head was the fact the highway that went through their town was gone, replaced with a dirt road.

Not one person came out as they drove toward the sheriff's office.

Lilly pointed to an intersection. "Pull over here. I want to see if Emma is okay." She took off the motorcycle helmet as he pulled over to the side, followed by Running Wolf.

"Which house is hers?" Dark Horse got off the bike, scanning around them as his men spread out.

"The green one with the white shutters. Do you know if her father made it?" Lilly refused to look at the man. If he didn't want to answer her questions, then screw him.

Men moved around the house in question, before Dark Horse wrapped his arm around her and tugged on her hair till she had no choice to stare up into his dark eyes.

"I know you're hurt right now, but this is not the time or place to discuss this and we will discuss this need of yours." He placed a kiss on her nose then moved her toward the house.

Before they reached the porch steps, Lilly glanced up at the side window and saw Emma peeking through the curtain, tears running down her cheeks.

"I see her, but we need to make sure no one is in there with her. Wait," Dark Horse whispered against the side of her head.

Running Wolf and Kizzy moved up beside them. Tears ran down Kizzy's face as well. "Her father is dead inside. That sheriff did this. They were searching for Emma, but she was well hidden. Her father saved her."

The front door opened, and one of Dark Horse's men stood behind Emma as she ran out the door, flying into Lilly's arms, crying, "They killed Papa. He made me promise to stay in the hiding place when they came. I should have helped."

"Then you would both be dead. Now you live on, giving your father the one thing he wanted more than life, your safety." Dark Horse ran his hand down the girl's head. "Do you have any other family we can take you to?"

Emma shook her head. "They killed Momma and Papa. They were all I had." Emma peered up at Lilly. "Where do I go?"

"You stay with me. We'll get through this together Emma. My father is waiting for us back at our new home."

Dark Horse took a deep breath and nodded before glancing at the road.

"Emma, we're going to put you in the van with Kizzy's brother. I want you to stay in there till we head back to our new home. The only time you come out of that van is if one of us comes to you, or

Mason tells you to." He glanced down at the girl. "Right now is a very dangerous time, so will you listen?"

Emma squeezed Lilly tight, nodding. "I'll do whatever you say," she whispered. "You really want me to stay with you?" Emma held onto Lilly tight.

"Yes, and my father will want you with us, also. You will always have a home with us." Lilly hugged the girl before turning and moving with her down the sidewalk. The van pulled up, but Lilly stopped, seeing the one person she never wanted to see again, Fuzz.

Before Lilly could say a word, Running Wolf wrapped his arm around Emma, Lilly and Kizzy, guiding them toward the van as she watched Dark Horse and the others spread out.

"But, he..." Lilly started to say something, but Running Wolf squeezed her shoulder and shook his head as the van side door opened.

Emma and Kizzy jumped into the van as Lilly watched. Dark Horse gave her a possessive look that sent shivers down her spine. He was claiming her right there in front of Fuzz, making sure he watched. "Get inside, *my little flower*," he emphasized the word my and his nickname for her before turning his attention back to her worse nightmare, Fuzz.

"Lilly." Running Wolf helped her into the van then closing the door. "You know where to take them,"

The van took off, and he joined Dark Horse.

She hated to admit it, but right now Lilly was more afraid then she had been before. The thought of something happening to Dark Horse... Her stomach seemed to want to reject her food from that morning, but she kept it down. Yet, she couldn't stop the shaking of her hands as she tucked them under her legs.

"Don't they know they have guns? They're just standing there out in the open," Lilly growled, staring out the window. She swore it appeared like one of those old movies shootouts.

Mason laughed. "You have nothing to worry about. Even if this creep pulled a gun, he'd be dead in seconds," Mason informed her just as tire popped on the van, sending them all to the side. "Get down, all of you," Mason ordered as he drove the van toward the sheriff's office.

Lilly covered Emma's body, Kizzy lying next to her in the back of the van. "I should have come out and let them have me. My father would be alive, and you would be safe," Emma cried.

"Afraid not, Emma." Lilly kissed the top of her head. "Fuzz and his gang had my father and I trapped at our home. I was lucky he agreed to let my father go to the hospital, but I paid the price for it. He wants me back, Emma, so you are not the only one this thing wants. But he won't get us. I won't allow him that ever again." Mason took the van around the corner quickly, almost tipping over.

"Get by the door. When I turn us around, we are going to make a run for the sheriff's office," Mason yelled out.

Lilly lifted her head. "Are you sure it's safe? They knew we would be coming, Mason. Something isn't right."

"I feel it, too. Something is off," Kizzy echoed her worries as Mason whipped the van around in front of the sheriff's office.

Lilly shoved Emma toward Kizzy then opened the door to the van and jumped out before they could stop her, slamming the door shut. Proving to them it was a trap, making sure not one of them would get hurt because of her.

But Lilly didn't even get to turn around as three burning slugs entered her body. She fell to her knees, clutching the van door, in worse pain than after the beating she had taken. Hot liquid she knew had to be blood dripped down her back.

She rested her forehead on the cool van, blackness threating to take her away. "Sorry, my Dark Warrior, so sorry," she whispered, tears rolling down her cheeks as she released the van door, allowing the darkness to take the pain away.

Chapter Eleven

There are two great days in a person's life—the day we are born and the day we discover why.
William Barclay

Dark Horse's his legs gave out, pain radiating throughout his body like he'd never felt before. Their target, Fuzz, was gone like the wind, and he knew in his heart Lilly was fading from this world.

"Lilly," he growled, forcing himself to stand, knowing the pain wasn't his, but his light, his little flower.

With his strength returning, Dark Horse ran to his metal horse with one purpose, to save the one who already carried his dark heart in her hands. *"Sorry, my Dark Warrior, so sorry."* Her pain-filled voiced ripped through his head and heart, shredding everything he had in him as he raced toward the sheriff's office.

What Dark Horse saw as he turned the curve had his heart in his throat. His Lilly lay on the ground, her blond hair spread out, soaking up her blood as Red Hawk hovered over her. Kizzy held Lilly's head in her lap.

Kizzy's tearful gaze lifted to his as he turned off his bike, moving to her side, dropping to his knees beside her. "Red Hawk?"

"Find the bastard who did this, because, Dark Horse, she's lucky the bullets weren't an inch to the right or she wouldn't be walking again much less breathing. She has died twice Dark Horse. I have one more bullet to take out of her, but it's very close to her heart. Take Kizzy's place. I need you to call to her, Dark Horse, hold her to you. I've kept her alive so far with Kizzy's help, but she needs you," Red Hawk stared to work on her again without waiting.

Dark Horse didn't know what he was saying, but he slipped in where Kizzy had been, placing Lilly's head on his lap. "I'm here, little flower. You didn't listen, did you?" He ignored those around him, knowing Running Wolf and his men would cover them, seeking those that had done this, holding those they caught for him. "You can't leave, my little flower. Only you can give me the peace I need to survive. I know you hear me Lilly. Don't forget, we have Emma to take care. I can't do it alone. She needs you. Hell, we all do." He leaned down, placing a kiss on her cheek.

Red Hawk laid his hand over the last hole in her back, his hands covered in Lilly's blood. Dark Horse swore he saw sparks coming from him, and heat spread out as Red Hawk held his hands over her wound, his eyes closed, concentrating.

Holding onto Lilly, Dark Horse never believe he could feel this way about anyone, but he had been wrong Lilly whimpered, and it broke his heart.

"Hold her down. Don't let her move," Red Hawk ground out, not opening his eyes. Sweat rolled down his face as he lifted his hand up. Lilly's body twitched under him as he held her down, watching as Red Hawk lowered his hand down and dug his fingers into the whole in her back, pulling the bullet out of her body.

Her chest rose, and then there was nothing. "Lilly, don't you dare leave me!" Dark Horse growled then leaned down to her ear. "I mean it, little flower. I can't be without you, please." A single tear rolled down his face and dropped onto Lilly's cheek. He had never cried since his mother's death. "See? Only you bring me to tears, baby. Only you and Momma." He buried his face into her hair, closing his eyes, his heart in his throat as time stood still. More tears rolled down his face onto her.

A soft small hand reached down and squeezed his shoulder.

"Look," Emma whispered, next to him. "She's moving her hand."

Dark Horse lifted his head as she tried to push Red Hawk away. His friend opened his eyes and smiled at him. "She is a fighter but it's going to take me a few sessions to heal her fully. We need to get her out of here now, while we can. Jay Bird grab the board that is tied to the side of the van, also those two blankets from the back. Once I get her in the van, I need to peel this jacket and shirt off of her that remains, and clean the wounds before I heal her," his friend ordered, covering the last hole in her back with gauze just like the other two. "And Lilly, I know you can hear me. You do not move when we lift you. You allow us to do this. You should know the routine."

"Shouldn't we take her to the hospital?" Emma asked Dark Horse, while Red Hawk, Running Wolf all carefully slid the board under his woman, covering her body with one of the blankets.

"No, Emma, it's Red Hawk destiny to heal our Lilly. She would have died if we left it up to the doctors." Running Wolf's attention moved to him as they carried Lilly to the van.

"You believe it's his destiny to heal our women?" Dark Horse scanned the area.

"Yes, I do. The sheriff has been caught with another. But I'm afraid this Fuzz sacrificed the sheriff to get away," he growled.

"As soon as Lilly is settled and I know she is safe, I'm going hunting. I'm done waiting for him to come to us. Lilly needs to know she's safe, not hunted," he glanced inside the van as Red Hawk worked at cutting off her clothes. "I'll be right behind you. Emma, get in the van with Lilly."

Mason walked up to him. "I'm sorry, Dark Horse. This never should have happened. I failed to protect your woman." His head hung low as he stared down at the ground.

"Did you know this was going to happen? Did you know they were there?" He frowned and turned toward the sheriff's office. "Where are the two police officers who came in from Dangerfield?"

Dark Horse slid his knife from his pants as Mason, Jay Bird, and Running Wolf turned their attention to the jail. "Two Eyes get the van out of here now." Using sign language, Running Wolf order half of their men to the back off the office. Dark Horse slammed the door.

Anger, the need to kill those that had harmed Lilly pulsed through him like that of an extra heart, beating loud and strong. Jay Bird moved to the left, Mason to the right, as they headed right through the front doors.

He glanced at Running Wolf and mouthed, who? Wanting to know who of theirs was supposed to be there helping out. Running Wolf signaled two of Raining Song's men, meaning that two of his men were either missing, or dead.

For their sakes, they'd better be dead, because they could have warned them and saved Lilly from such a horrible fate. But then again, it was part of their destiny, one that sucked big time. Either way, they better be dead he thought.

The smell of death filled the air around them as they slid inside without a sound, and what greeted them was not a pretty site.

Blood soaked the walls and the floors. The heads of the two police officers were sitting on the desk placed right in front, sending them a message. Their eyes were gone, and each head had a name carved on it, *Dark Horse* and *Running Wolf.*

The two men came through the back stopped at the hallway, shaking their heads, indicating there was no one else in the building. "Just for the sake of it see if there are any recordings of what happened in here," Dark Horse ordered the two. "Jay Bird, contact Raining Song and find out if he has heard from his men, but make sure you don't accuse him of anything, since we know he's supposed to be with us."

Mason shook his head. "Now I know why Kizzy and Lilly didn't want to come in here. They both knew something was wrong as soon as we turned the corner," Mason snarled. "You think they had help?"

"Don't you? Weren't the feds supposed to show up today?" Dark Horse asked, Running Wolf who was already pulling his phone out and dialing his friend.

Dark Horse inched around the main room, searching for clues as to where Raining Song's men had gone, but there was nothing. Almost as if... "I can't believe I didn't see this before." Dark Horse glanced over at Running Wolf. "All of this has been staged. It's clean as a whistle except for that the blood splatter."

"Tack has called his older brother Flynn, since the local FBI agents are missing also. Jay Bird, what did you find out?" Running Wolf joined him at the door.

"We should have followed the van," Dark Horse growled, heading straight toward his bike, seeing his tires slashed as were the others there.

All four of them, spread out, taking cover, searching for the ones who had done this, but they were silent nothing, as the sound of bikes reached them.

Running Wolf motioned for half their men to scout the area as he jumped on behind Sun Bull, and Dark Horse behind Night Wind, hating that for now they would leave their bikes. "Get me back to the house. Something isn't right," Dark Horse growled, hoping that his Lilly was safe, but his gut was telling him different.

***

Pain once more attacked her body, but she was alive, for now. Emma and Kizzy sat off to the side as someone placed their hand on her back. Intense heat soaked into her skin.

"Don't move, Lilly. I'm still healing you, and I don't need you to open what I've done. I'm Red Hawk. We met yesterday."

Wetting her lips, Lilly met Kizzy's gaze. "We have bigger problems right now, Red Hawk. They're coming." At once the heat was gone and Red Hawk scooted back. She knew he was staring out the back window, when he started to cuss.

"There is an old abandoned place up a head, we'll have to make a stand there," the driver yelled.

"Lilly cannot be jarred right now. Get the others to cover us when we carry her in, Two Eyes," Red Hawk snapped.

Lilly took a deep breath. "Stop the van and let me out, and you all go. You know he wants me."

Kizzy placed her hand on her shoulder. "Do not move. We are not going anywhere. You are not sacrificing yourself for any of us." Kizzy bent down, her gaze meeting hers. "Believe me, I know how you feel, but these men won't hear of it, and it will just piss them off more. You really don't want Dark Horse mad, he's already close to the edge, right?"

The van stopped. "I should be able to help," Lilly mumbled as the door opened next to her.

"You do help, Lilly. You're Dark Horse's reason for going on," the driver, Two Eyes told her. He helped Red Hawk lift the board she was on, moving into a small, almost empty storefront. Kizzy and Emma ran in front of them, crouching down behind an old freezer.

Lowering her to the floor, Red Hawk leaned over and whispered. "We have plenty of men to keep them at bay till the others show up. Your job is to stay still and rest."

, Red Hawk and Two Eyes moved to the front of the store, waiting when she felt a small, cold hand slide into hers, Emma. The girl smiled at her, trying to be strong, but fear filled her gaze. "*He'll come,*" she mouthed to the little girl, but did she really believe his promise?

Lilly couldn't blame him on the shooting. A sharpshooter could take out anyone.

"Down," Red Hawk yelled right before an explosion rattled the building and shattered windows.

"All those things that were in there," Emma whispered, glancing up to where they had come.

"We can replace things, Emma, but we can't replace you," Lilly mumbled and coughed.

Kizzy nodded and squeezed her shoulder right before bullets started to hit the sides of the building.

"You know, I'm so glad I didn't join the army like I was planning to." Lilly tried to smile. Kizzy and Emma lay plastered on the floor next to her. "I think we're going to have to come up with some major protection for these tunnels they're searching for, because after this..."

"I think a few tigers to prowl around would be nice," Kizzy growled.

Emma smiled. "How about a moat with alligators in it?"

"Hell, we're going to have to get that special bulletproof glass, too," Lilly grumbled as a few shots flew over their heads, coming close. "I think it's time Dad called some of his army friends and start gathering stuff."

A few minutes after the shots started to die down, Emma started to lift her head, but Lilly tugged her down again. "Don't. They can be waiting for us to move." She tried to forget about the new pain in her lower calf, from what she had no idea.

"Soon, ladies. Our men are starting to pick a few of them off, and I hear bikes coming," Two Eyes yelled to them. "You okay back there?"

"I think I was hit in the thigh, and if I'm not mistaken Lilly was hit again," Kizzy growled.

She sighed, "Yeah, lower calf, but it's not like I'm not in pain anyway. Just call me a human pin cushion."

"I know we could get a metal detector." Emma smiled at her.

"I'm afraid that wouldn't work. Every warrior would set it off with the knives and things they carry." Lilly grunted, when she felt someone behind her.

"Easy, it's me. I want to check you both out. Dark Horse and Running Wolf are out there, so we're safe for now." Red Hawk carefully turned her leg. "A piece of wood caught you from where the bullet hit, sending it up in the air. Hold still while I pull this out and then I'll check on Kizzy."

"I hate to say this, but why does it seem they have more men than we thought?" Kizzy growled, what she had been thinking.

"That's because they do, and from what I've seen out the window it's someone that shouldn't be there." Red Hawk yanked the piece of wood out of her leg.

"Fuck that hurt," she snapped and tried to lift up, but another hand held her down.

"Don't move, little flower, and watch the mouth. It's too pretty to be sprouting such ugliness." Dark Horse's voice was like a calming balm to her nerves.

"You're okay?" she wanted to see him.

"Two Eyes, grab the first aid kit out of Dark Horse's bike," Red Hawk yelled.

"You'll have to use Night Wing's. My bike is back in town with two sliced tires as is Running Wolf's," Dark Horse growled.

"Damn it, I hate lying here," Lilly snarled. Two seconds later, Dark Horse was leaning over her, placing a kiss on her cheek.

"You will do as Red Hawk says. I lost you once, little flower. I will not lose you again. I don't like being scared, and you scared the living shit out of me. We will be speaking about your need to place yourself in danger later." He nipped her earlobe.

"There is nothing to talk about. I wasn't about to let anything happen to Kizzy or Emma. Plus, I really didn't think it would be that bad." Lilly took a deep breath as Dark Horse reached over and squeezed Emma's shoulder.

"You have done really good, not panicking. I'm proud of you, Emma, and glad to have you in our family. When it's safe, we'll go back to your home and collect what you want, but first we get rid of this threat hanging over us." Dark Horse took the first aid kit from Two Eyes and handed it to Red Hawk who now worked on Kizzy's leg.

"I'm afraid you got that bullet, Kizzy." Red Hawk dug in the first aid kit as Running Wolf joined them, kneeling down next to his wife.

"We have any alive?" Dark Horse asked as she felt a cool wet cloth on her leg.

"Three, and one of them was at breakfast yesterday morning." Running Wolf's gaze met hers.

Lilly heard Dark Horse jump up behind her, the cool cloth gone from her leg. "He's a dead man."

"Sit down and take care of your woman. We will get our women home safe, healed, and secure, then we'll deal with the traitors our way." Running Wolf smiled, but it wasn't a good smile. A shiver went down her spine.

"You are right, but I hate leaving them to breath the same air we are," Dark Horse grumbled, sitting back down and taking her leg, gently cleaning it. "We have another van coming, but it won't be here for a little bit."

"Not to mention Stephan is beyond furious," Running Wolf grunted, making Kizzy groan as her brother came around the corner.

"What the hell happened?" Mason slid in behind Running Wolf. "You're so not going anywhere again," Mason growled, watching Red Hawk pull out the bullet.

"Shut the fuck up," Kizzy snapped. "Why is every time we get hurt they start throwing out more stupid rules." Kizzy rolled her eyes, causing Emma to giggle.

"Don't think I know you just rolled those eyes," Mason grumbled.

Running Wolf shook his head. "Enough, you two. How is she, Red Hawk?"

"I got the bullet out and shut the wound, but she'll be sore for a few days. I could heal it fully, but I need to do another round on Lilly's back." Red Hawk sat back on his butt and she saw how tired he was.

"I can wait a few hours. Maybe you need to rest? For a dark man, you appear a little white there," Lilly smiled at the amazing man, Red Hawk with a truly gods-given gift. "You'll have to explain to me later how your gifts work and how you brought me back because I know for a fact I shouldn't be talking to you right now."

Red Hawk put a thick pad of gauze on Kizzy's wound. "There are many things in the world that we can't explain. My talent is one of those things." Red Hawk sat back against the wall, again. "Kizzy will be fine. Keep a bandage on it and the leg up when we get them back to the house," Red Hawk informed Running Wolf, before turning back to her. "I really didn't know about my gift till I was about seven. It feels like another lifetime."

Lilly frowned. "Red Hawk you don't have to tell me if you don't want to. I didn't mean to pry, I was just curious, well because being an RN, I know what you did was a miracle to me."

"It is to me, too, each time I help someone, like Kizzy and you. But the first time it scared the living crap out of me. If it wasn't for Soaring Eagle, I think I would have gone crazy." He shook his head and took a deep breath.

"You really don't have to explain." Dark Horse took her shoes off and proceeded to rub her feet.

"No, I don't mind, anyway, and we have time. As I was saying, I was seven when there was an accident on the reservation. We had been having massive rains, and the roofs of one of the stores had collapsed. I was across the street running an errand for my mother when it happened. People were coming out of the place crying, blood all over them, but when they brought out the owner, Mr. Wess, my whole body started to burn, almost as if I was being led across the street by some unseen hand." He glanced back at her and smiled. "You know what the weirdest thing was?"

She frowned. "What?"

"That it seemed everyone around me knew I could help him. They moved out of the way as I made my way to him. Pulsing energy was coursing through me. I'm surprised it didn't fry my brain. But as soon as I touched Mr. Wess, it was like I was in a small tunnel, traveling through his body to the areas that need the most help. I don't know how long I was kneeling beside him when I felt a firm hand on my shoulder. Soaring Eagle caught me when I would have fallen over from exhaustion. It's not like surgery, more like intense heat surrounding the injured part, if that makes sense."

"Impressive. Makes total sense, really. It's one of our bodies' ways of healing themselves. There are many cases of small incidents of this healing, and it has to do with the fingertips and a warming sensation. Well, I thank you for saving me." She tried to move just a little and heard the growls.

"Let's get this second healing done so I don't have to worry about you moving." Red Hawk came over to her and pulled the blankets down to expose her back.

"Sorry. I always did have trouble holding still, even when I was small. It drove my dad crazy," Lilly smiled. "I guess it's Dark Horse's time to go crazy."

Kizzy laughed, glancing behind her. "I have to admit I might have the same problem."

"Might? You do, and I'm beginning to think the possible solution is to handcuff your cute butt to our bed, but I know our daughter needs you," Running Wolf grumbled.

"I have a few pairs of handcuffs that would work nicely on you, little flower. Matter of fact, I picked up a new pair on the way here." Dark Horse moved to her other side, whispering in her ear, "Now, be a good pet. I'd hate to have to spank this cute butt when before I have the chance to worship it." Dark Horse placed his hand on her ass.

Chapter Twelve

If you know the enemy and know yourself you need not fear the results of a hundred battles.

Sun Tzu

Dark Horse got in the back of the van, sitting next to Lilly who had finally fallen asleep after Red Hawk's last healing session.

Red Hawk was resting against the side of the van next to her as they headed back toward their temporary home.

He smiled, brushing her hair away from her face. His little flower hadn't mumbled a word after Dark Horse had informed her what he couldn't wait to do. Yes, one day soon he would be burying his cock in her ass, but first he would claim his Lilly, making her his body and soul.

"You keep staring at me like that, I'm going to burn up." She smiled at him. "Do you think Dad's okay? What if they went after them, too?"

He leaned down, placing a kiss on her cheek. "Your father is fine. I spoke with Stephan before we left. They are waiting for us and have security all around the property. They're safe."

"Why did that group join with Fuzz? You would think they'd hate anything to do with him."

"We don't know yet, but we'll find out. Not to worry. For them to totally ignore what the Great Mother is saying, well there hasn't to be something we are missing. But I don't want you to worry about it. We'll figure it out soon."

"We didn't get to help the townsfolk like I wanted. Hell, I didn't see anyone except for Emma." She frowned. "You don't think they have enough men to take the town again, do you?" Lilly tried to rise up, but he held her down.

"Calm down, Lilly. They aren't going to take the town. Our men are there now, along with the federal agents we called in. Believe me, right now, your town has so many FBI agents crawling around, not even this Fuzz is going to want to show his face, let alone these men."

She let out the breath she'd been holding. "You're going after him, aren't you?"

Red Hawk was staring at him. "Yes, as soon as I get you tucked into our bed, fed, and make sure our new place is secure," he told her.

"And you're going with him?" Kizzy sat next to Emma, staring at Running Wolf.

"Yes, they shot at my woman. It's time to revert to the old days. Plus, you double-cross us, it's the last time you will hurt anyone. But I have a feeling the Great Mother might beat us to the punch on some of the men."

Dark Horse couldn't help but growl. "I hope she leaves me Fuzz. We already have the sheriff. I have plans for each one."

"So much anger. Tell me, did this Fuzz do something to you?" Lilly peered up at him and covering his hand with hers. "Because you don't need to do anything dangerous for me. Matter of fact, I'd rather you wouldn't. If something were to happen..."

Dark Horse knelt down so his nose was touching hers. "Nothing is going to happen to me or Running Wolf, and you alone are enough reason for this hunt, but there are things going on here. You will not worry about this, little flower. The only thing I want you to do is rest and get well, because I have a night out planned for the two of us when this is done. Have you ever been to New Orleans?"

When her eyes got all big, he smiled.

"But do we have time? There's so much to do," Lilly frowned and he could see the wheels turning.

Dark Horse kissed her because he had no choice. "Two nights will not make a difference, and I truly believe you deserve those nights. My gift to you, our wedding."

"Our what?" Lilly sputtered and glared at him. "I've known you two days and you're planning our marriage without even asking me?"

He couldn't but help laugh at her expression. "Yes, your father has already given you to me, and I'm keeping you."

"You can't keep people, Dark Horse," Lilly growled, glaring at him. Behind him he heard giggling and turned his gaze on Emma.

"And what are you laughing at young lady? Remember you'll be living with us, and just wait till those boys start lining up." Dark Horse pulled out his smaller knife, staring at Emma the whole time.

"You can't be serious?" Emma squeaked and peeked around him. "He's not serious, is he?"

"I have a feeling he's very serious, but two heads are better than one, I'm thinking, when it comes to this man," Lilly said.

"I accept the challenge and don't worry, I'm quite ready for the job for both of you." Dark Horse smiled.

"Don't worry. You are not the only one who is going to have trouble when our daughter gets older," Kizzy grumbled, facing Running Wolf.

"There will be no trouble. Our daughter isn't setting foot out of our home unless I approve of who she is with. Simple." He shrugged.

"Why do I get the feeling he's going to be worse than my father was?" Emma groaned.

Dark Horse laughed and patted her leg. "Not to worry. We'll take good care of you."

The van slowed, drawing his attention.

"What is it?" They were still a few miles from their home base.

"It seems that we have company, um the good kind," Jay Bird turned and nodded to the car in front of them on the side of the road. "Looks like your friend from Ohio has found his way here."

Sliding between the seats, Dark Horse laughed and shook his head. "I should have known Tack wouldn't allow a little thing like states stop him from coming and getting in on some of the action."

Running Wolf smacked him on the shoulder. "He reminds me of you so much, but more controlled. At least that was what I thought. But then again, if his brother is here, of course Tack would come.

Dark Horse grunted as Jay Bird pulled over to the side of the road. Opening the side door, he glanced at Lilly. "I can't wait for you to meet Tack. Next to Running Wolf, Tack is one of my best friends and one of the best detectives around. He and his brother are both here to help us, and it seems they have brought friends too." He reached over and squeezed her foot. "I'll be right back."

Jumping out of the van, Dark Horse heard Kizzy grumbling. "That's what you call male bonding. I'm surprised they don't take off their shirts and beat their chests."

Dark Horse grinned at Running Wolf who was getting out of the van. "Sounds like someone needs a little attention when we get back."

Running Wolf smiled. The heated stare he gave his wife would make anyone hot. "And I will make sure to take care of that, too."

"What? You will not touch my ass again. It's still sore from the last spanking you gave me," she snapped.

Running Wolf snorted and moved beside him, meeting Tack and his brother Flynn, shaking their hands.

"Does your boss know you're here?" Dark Horse asked, hugging the man he considered a brother of the heart.

"I gave my notice. Since my friends and family are here. I'll be staying here with you and Flynn, helping where I can," Tack slapped his back.

"It's about time my little brother came home. I have fifteen of my men now joining yours, going through the town. We will get these pieces of shit soon," Flynn snapped.

Tack raised his eyebrows then glanced behind him. "Is that Lilly?"

"It better not be, or she's going to have a sore damn ass," Dark Horse turned to see her standing there with Red Hawk frowning down at her as he held her up.

Dark Horse took a deep breath, moving toward his stubborn woman. "Red Hawk just healed you. What do you think you are doing?" He wrapped his arm around her other side.

She leaned close to him and whispered. "Pee. I have to pee." Lilly scanned around, biting her lip, holding the blanket to her front.

"Tack, Flynn, meet my lady. Lilly, these gentlemen will be with us and helping us. If you'll excuse us for a minute, gentlemen, Running Wolf will explain our plans." Dark Horse moved off the road heading toward a few boulders. He guided them around so she would be covered but heard the rattle and her whimper.

As if on auto pilot, Dark Horse sent his knife flying at the same time Red Hawk did, both blades sinking into the copperhead in front of them.

He turned his gaze on Lilly. She was staring down at the ground, not even looking at the snake, but at the puddle between her legs, tears running down her cheeks.

His heart broke as he carefully, gathered her into his arms while, Red Hawk grabbed their knives. "I'll give you two, sometime." He set his knife on the boulder, taking the snake and his knife. "Lilly you are going to get sick if you don't stop. I mean, it's only natural after what your body has gone through. Now, come on. Let's strip you down, and you can put on my shirt. It will cover you totally. When we get back to the house, I'll help you in the shower, so you're nice and clean."

Lilly wiped away the tears. "I feel like a little kid. Every time I turn around, you are having to help me with something." She clutched the blanket while he cut away her pants and underclothes.

Dark Horse glanced at Lilly as he pulled the clothes from her body, before stripping out of his shirt. "I was going to wait to explain a few things, but maybe now is a good time for this. Little flower, come on. Let me see those pretty eyes." Dark Horse waited till her gaze met his.

She took a deep breath.

"Lilly, I'm different from others. I'm going to need to take care of you. Sometimes, I'll give you your baths or feed you. I'll be picking out most of clothes, too, but when you are sick or hurt I'm afraid, I'll do be doing everything for you. I'll need to make sure you are all right."

"Dark Horse you are going to have so much to do, don't you

think that is a bit much? As for being sick or hurt, I like when you take care of me, even if it's a little embarrassing." She whispered the last part.

He stood and stripped out of his shirt, carefully helping her put it on. "No Lilly. If anything, it will help me. You are the most important person in my life Lilly. I will trust no one with you except for my family, and even with them I'll have limits as to who I trust you with. Because you are mine, Lilly, and I refuse to let you go." He carefully lifted her up into his arms, knowing she couldn't walk. After putting his knife away, placing a kiss on her lips. "Mine."

Lilly shook her head, before resting it on his shoulders. "Am I going to be your security blanket?" She kissed his chest.

"No, little flower, I'm going to be yours. Your everything." He placed her on the cushioned seat next to Kizzy, covering her legs with a clean blanket Red Hawk handed him. "Don't move till we get home," he ordered, and she laughed, reaching out, touching his cheek.

"I'll try to follow your orders but can't promise," she teased him as he turned and nipped her finger.

He kissed her hard before turning to Red Hawk, who offered half of the long snake, but Dark Horse shook his head. "You keep it and use it. You've done enough for us, and I know it can be used for other things."

"Thank you. It won't go to waste." Red Hawk stuffed the snake into his pouch at his hip before moving away. "She'll need one more healing when we get back to the house, but I'll wait till she gets cleaned up, because it's going to knock her out," his friend said as Running Wolf climbed into the van.

"Tack and Flynn are following us back to the house with a few of their men." Running Wolf closed the van door, taking his seat. "It seems we're going to have a full war party tonight."

"War party?" Lilly questioned, frowning.

"Nothing for you to worry about. You'll be sound asleep," Dark Horse told her, sitting at her feet.

Chapter Thirteen

In three words I can sum up everything I've learned about life: it goes on.

Robert Frost

Lilly stared up at the ceiling of the bedroom and sighed. It was after two in the morning, Dark Horse and the others still hadn't gotten back. Oh, Red Hawk had been right about her sleeping after he healed her again, but that had lasted a total of five hours before her eyes popped open.

"Well I can't just lie here," she grumbled and moved to the edge of the bed, shoving the covers off of her naked body. Never had Lilly slept in the nude, but Dark Horse had given her another one of his silly rules, that she would always be naked in bed.

He had told her that little bit of information in the shower as he had held onto her, cleaning every inch of her body. By the time the shower was over, her body was humming with need, but Dark Horse refused to give her what she craved, telling her not yet.

"The big jerk," Lilly mumbled, slowly getting up heading for the T-shirt she had tried to put on earlier, but he had thrown it across the room. Slowly, she bent down grabbing the T-shirt and sighing when all Lilly felt was a little pull in her back. Yes, Red Hawk was a miracle worker. She would have to do something special for him before he left, and Lilly knew exactly what it was. Cleo.

A soft knock had Lilly turning to her door as she pulled the T-shirt down, covering herself, when Kizzy poked her head in.

"Thought I heard you moving around. Couldn't sleep either?"

Lilly took the robe took the back of the door, before moving out of the bedroom, following Kizzy to the living room, where a small light was on. "Want to join me in having a night cap while we wait?" Kizzy held up the bottle of whiskey, and Lilly smiled.

"Now you are talking. Have you heard anything?" Lilly asked, going into the kitchen for a glass, and flinching a little when she reached up to grab one.

"I swear I should beat both of your asses," Stephan grumbled, coming into the kitchen from the back door. "Go sit down. I'll bring you a cup, but you are both going to eat a sandwich, too. You both ate nothing earlier," he grumbled.

Lilly was really getting to like Kizzy's uncle. "Thank you, I could eat now. Have you heard anything from anyone?" She joined Kizzy by the fireplace.

"No, and that has me worried. Someone should have checked in by now. I don't care how intense their war party was, you always let your backup know what the hell is going on." Stephan started making them sandwiches as Soaring Eagle came in shaking his head.

"You make enough noise to wake the dead. They are fine and will be home soon. I'll take a sandwich, too, since you are making them." Soaring Eagle faced her. "So, how are you feeling?"

"A little sore, but otherwise just wired. So much going through my mind, and everything is so..." Lilly blew out a breath.

"Overwhelming. Tell me about it. The thought that we are to try and save thousands." Kizzy swirled the drink in her hand before taking a sip.

"Others will survive. It won't be just our group. The Great

Mother won't call all her children home." Soaring Eagle stretched his legs out in front of him, sitting next to her on the couch. "I heard you and Dark Horse are going to New Orleans next week. Are you ready to commit to my son fully? Or did he just order you to do it?" He smiled. "My son has a way with words, I'm afraid."

Lilly and Kizzy both snorted, and she took a sip of whiskey, allowing it to burn down her throat before answering. "Of course, he ordered, just like he has done most of the time I've been with him." She glanced at Soaring Eagle. "But in a lot of ways he reminds me of my father," she smiled. "My father was always telling my mother, instead of asking her, and even did it to me. So, I guess I'm kind of used to this kind of personality trait, but his proposal or order to marry him was different for sure. Haven't decided to ignore it or what." Lilly rested her head back against the small couch. "How can one feel so comfortable with someone you just met? Even with my father's approval of Dark Horse, there is a small part that is afraid." She looked over at Kizzy. "What if I'm just leaning on him because I don't want to be hurt again? How do I know it's going to last? We don't even know each other." She sighed and took another sip of her drink.

"Do you know it's only been a month since Running Wolf and I got married? Well, technically it will be on Tuesday. We only knew each other two days also, but I have to say I wouldn't change a day of what we have had. Now, I might limit his damn spankings, but already I know he's my heart and my soul." Kizzy leaned over and placed her hand on her knee.

"I have a feeling with these men any woman who joins with them is not going to get the normal courting, dates and such. There just isn't the time. They are living for the day, wanting to give us everything they can for now because when things go out of control it's going to be bad."

"That is one of the reasons I'm seriously considering this." She smiled. "And the fact the man is...well, damn."

Kizzy laughed, and Soaring Eagle grinned. "Yes, my sons, all of them are strong and independent. Each of them could hold their own with the coming battle we will be facing, but having four stations in the states, we'll be able to save more people." Soaring Eagle sighed.

Lilly reached over. "You're upset about Raining Song. I still don't understand why he'd join forces with the bikers. It just does not make sense."

"It does in some ways. I have a feeling he believed if he joined with this Fuzz now, he'd gain control of the area after the destruction, that the Great Mother would take care of the bikers herself, leaving him in charge of this area. I'm just sorry for Black Bull. He and Raining Song were close from what I had heard," Soaring Eagle explained to her.

"Do you think Black Bull is working with him also?" Lilly tapped her fingers on the side of the couch.

"No, Black Bull found out the hard way, I'm afraid, about his friend," Dark Horse came into the room, the clothes he'd worn replaced by others. His hair was damp and pulled back like he had taken a shower.

She started to get up, but Dark Horse pushed back into her seat, sitting on the arm of the couch next to her. "We found Black Bull had already cornered Raining Song. It was sad, but the Great Mother took him home along with the few who had joined him."

"What about the sheriff and Fuzz?" Lilly was almost afraid of the answer.

"I wouldn't be back if they weren't taken care of, little flower. They will not be bothering anyone again." Dark Horse glanced up as Running Wolf came into the room, carrying plates of food, with Stephan behind him.

"It's time to put all of this behind us and concentrate on the problems coming our way." Running Wolf handed Kizzy and Lilly each a plate, while Stephan passed one to Soaring Eagle.

"Would you two care for something?" Stephan asked.

"No, we're fine, but why are you up, little flower?" Dark Horse leaned closer to her.

"You really have to ask?" she mumbled around the best roast beef sandwich Lilly had had in a long while.

Running Wolf laughed as did Dark Horse. "Is the sandwich that good?" He glanced from her to Kizzy.

"Leave her alone. It's probably the first time she's actually tasting the food and breathing," Kizzy grumbled, peeking up at Running Wolf. "You know."

Running Wolf lifted Kizzy and took her seat as, Dark Horse did the same, placing Lilly in his lap, wrapping his arms around her. "Now I wish I'd had steaks ready for you," Dark Horse grumbled, "but we'll have those in New Orleans, I promise."

"That's my cue to go and try and get some sleep," Soaring Eagle stood and stretched. "We'll see you in the morning, but not too early." He headed toward the back where he was staying with her father.

"I'm off to take care of our lady's gentlemen. They are special." Stephan kissed Kizzy's cheek then shocked her by coming over to kiss hers. "What you don't think you're part of the family? Think again Lilly."

Stephan patted Dark Horse on the shoulder and headed toward the back door to where he was staying with his brother in the camper they had brought.

She faced Dark Horse. "He's really gone, Fuzz, the sheriff?"

"Yes, Lilly, and I'm not telling you the details. You have suffered enough. Just know you can rest, little flower," Dark Horse reassured her as she shivered at the expression that came over him.

Lilly knew she'd never ask what happened. Her nightmare was really over. He had done what he had promised her. Dark Horse was truly her Dark Knight as he'd called himself, earlier. She reached up and pulled him down, kissing his lips. "Thank you," she whispered as a tear rolled down her cheek.

"There is no need to thank me. I promised you I would always take care of you, little flower, and I will." He smiled. "Did I hear you were considering marrying me? If I'm not mistaken, I didn't ask."

Lilly laughed. She couldn't help it. "That you did, but that does not mean I'm going to listen, now, does it?" She took a bite of the pickle Stephan had put on her plate. "Mmm, I love garlic dill pickles."

Kizzy giggled. "They're my favorite, too. So, when are you planning this trip?"

"Nosey little thing, aren't you?" Running Wolf laughed. "We're going to my gypsy. We never did have a honeymoon, and they'll need us to stand up for them. Plus, we need to contact a few people." He kissed the top of Kizzy's head.

Kizzy rolled her eyes, stuffing a bite of her sandwich in her mouth. "Of course, you have other plans. It couldn't just be a simple wedding trip." She shook her head.

Lilly shrugged. "Any trip to New Orleans for business or pleasure would be fun. I've always wanted to go, but then I want to visit a few places. I think Greece and Ireland are the top two for overseas. I love anything to do with the Greek gods, but, alas that isn't going to happen in this life time." She smiled up at him.

"Never really thought about going overseas. Had no desire to. We have so many wonders here on this continent, I was content to travel it," Dark Horse nibbled at her neck.

"Stop, that tickles." Lilly popped the last bit of her sandwich in her mouth, moving her neck away from his mouth.

He put her plate on the coffee table before swinging her up in his arms. "My pickle." She tried to reach down to it and he snorted, bending so she could grab it.

"We'll see you in the morning. I have some pleasurable torture to hand out, it seems." Dark Horse carried her toward their bedroom.

"Can torture be pleasurable?" She munched on her pickle as he lowered her feet to the floor once they were inside their room.

"I know many forms of pleasurable torture and plan to use every one on you till I can get you to agree with me. Strip," he ordered, shutting the door with his foot, taking his shirt off, and throwing it to the floor.

"I have my pickle to finish," she squeaked and backed away from him, noticing his heated gaze, traveling up her body.

"Two minutes," he growled, never taking his gaze off her as she took a bit of her pickle. The juice ran down her cheek. But before she had a chance to wipe it away, he was there lowering his head, lapping up the juice.

"Never did like pickles, but on you, I might have to change my mind." He nipped at her bottom lip. "Finish."

Lilly popped the last bite into her mouth as he shoved off the robe, allowing it to fall on the floor, before reaching for her T-shirt. "I think I've already taken this off you once tonight, did I not?" He pulled it up over her head.

Lilly frowned. "I couldn't go out there naked."

"You shouldn't be out there anyway. You died yesterday Lilly." He cupped her cheek. "Your or my body needs to rest. Walking around is not resting."

"And pleasurable torture is?" She smiling up at him.

He swept her up into his arms and laid her in the center of the bed. "Oh yes, if done right." Dark Horse sucked her nipple into his mouth, nipping it before covering it with his amazing tongue.

She stiffened, almost afraid to accept the pleasure Dark Horse was giving her. Lilly reached out, to only have him back away from the bed, stripping out of the rest of his clothes.

He stood there, staring down at her. The full moon lit the room just enough so she could see his body and he could see hers, scars and all.

"Stop," he growled, bending down his nose almost touching hers. "Do not ever cover yourself from me." He sat down on the corner of the bed, taking her hand and placing a kiss on her palm.

"You're mine, little flower. Mine to stare at, touch, and love. Never hide anything from me. With the rough times we have coming I'm going to expect you to be thoroughly honest. If for one minute I believe you are keeping something from me, I will stop everything I'm doing, no matter how important it is to find out what my beautiful flower is not sharing with me."

"Now, that is downright silly. What if I want to surprise you for some reason, birthday or whatever? You can't know everything, and you are going to be needed by many, Dark Horse, even I realize this." Lilly reached up and brushed a strand of hair out of the face of the man who had the darkest eyes she had ever seen on anyone.

"That's for me to judge. Little flower, you are the most important thing in my life. You are the one who is going to keep me going, even when things appear to be at our worst. Now, that might seem a lot to you, but I'm only making three rules. Follow them, and we have no problems." He climbed onto the bed, covering her body with his, without putting any weight on her.

And god did the man have a body. There wasn't an ounce of fat on him. "And what would those three rules be, dear sir," she teased, but the pleasure in his gaze at those words had her moaning. "Not only are you all alpha, beat your fists on your chest, but you're a little kinky, too?" she moaned, but inside was as happy as could be.

He didn't say a word as he kissed and nipped a path down her body, watching her. "We're going to New Orleans, little flower." He kissed her belly button. "Maybe I'll have them put a nice ruby stud here before our wedding while we're there." He lifted and carefully turned her over onto her stomach.

Dark Horse hovered over her, his fingers tracing the many scars, including Fuzz's marking. "I know what I want back here." Dark Horse placed his hand over her lower back where Fuzz's name was, before reaching over to his pillow and dragging out the knife he had shown her before. The one he had picked up in the same store as her box. He placed the knife next to her so she could see it.

"I want this tattooed into your skin with my name here on the blade." Dark Horse ran his finger over the shiny cooper blade.

It was so shiny... "Dark Horse?" Lilly glanced over her shoulder at him.

"Yes, my Lilly, this is the knife that ended their lives, as it should be. This is all I will tell you about this night. Will you wear my mark?" he asked again.

She turned her head and gazed at the knife beside her. It was stunning, almost beautiful, but deadly. It only seemed fitting that the weapon that killed him was tattooed on her back under all the whip scars he had given her.

"Yes, Dark Horse, I'll carry your mark," she whispered, reaching out to touch the knife, but he covered her hand with his and brought it up to his mouth, kissing it.

"You are light, and this is dark. Never touch it, Lilly. Just know that it is here with me, protecting what is mine." He nipped her finger. "You're going to marry me, too, aren't you?"

"When are we leaving for New Orleans?"

Dark Horse sat back frowning at her. "Why? You should listen to me, Lilly. Don't you understand how dangerous it's going to be?"

Lilly took a deep breath, closing her eyes. She tried to swallow back the tears, but it didn't happen. Swinging her feet around, Lilly tried to get off the bed, but Dark Horse was there wrapping his arms around her and pulling her back down, holding her tight.

His body warm, his hold not hurting, but calming, yet she still trembled. "What did I say, little flower, that hurt you so much?" He rubbed her back as his leg slid on top of hers, holding her down.

Chapter Fourteen

*The tears of hurt are the most precious tear, for they only come
out when your hearts in despair. Bring those emotions out and let
them flow. For you know your inner pain will make you glow.*
Abira Mukherjee

Dark Horse held her trembling body as she buried her face into
his chest and cried, breaking his heart. He could handle anger and
uncertainty, but her tears were an altogether different matter.

He reached behind him grabbing a few Kleenexes. "Come on,
little flower. Tell me what I did," Dark Horse asked, leaned back to
wipe her face.

"Sex... Obey..." She took a deep breath. "Where is the love, Dark
Horse? You want to own me, for me to obey you..." She waved her
hand around. "And for kink, but nothing about love. Marriage is
love." Her lip trembled. "He took everything else from me, and now
you want that without the mention of love."

"little flower," he growled, wrapping his hand in her hair and
pulling her head back, so he would have her full attention.

"I have never loved a woman except for my mother and now
you. Little flower you are my heart, the one who holds the fate of this
body and old soul." He released her hair, hugging her tight to him.
"I'll try and tell you often, but I'm afraid I'm a man of showing then
speaking." He laughed. "You want to know when I realized I love
you?" He smiled down at her when she nodded.

"That letter you wrote back to me? The one claiming…"

Lilly reached up and covered his mouth, moaning and shaking her head. "But how can this be? Does one fall in love so quickly? How do I know it's not me being grateful for you saving me? I want this between us to be special, to go into a marriage I need to know inside here it's right." She placed her hand on his chest. "And not gratitude for saving me."

"We don't leave for another two days. These two days you will see the difference between gratitude and love. But for now, I'm going to show you how loving me is going to be," he growled, right before he covered her mouth, loving it with all that he had. Showing her how much his little flower was wrapped around his heart.

She tasted of honey and the wind. Her lips soft as the lily blossoms she was named after, would be bruised and swollen, but little flower would be truly loved this night.

For the rest of his life Dark Horse would show his flower the love he had for her, never giving her a reason think he didn't cherish her.

He broke the kiss, nipping her chin and moving to her neck. His flower had a spot right under the back of her ear where her body wakened and screamed with delight when touched. And he planned to awaken more than her body.

There would be no more memories of the monster who had hurt her, just Dark Horse. He scraped his teeth against the sensitive skin, feeling her nipples harden under him and a shiver run through her body as he sucked on the area, making sure he left his love mark on her.

Dark Horse's cock was hard and ready, but she wasn't as he sat up, cupping her lush full round breasts, squeezing and playing with her nipples, giving each one personal time.

Her body responded just as he knew it would, skin pink where he had left love bites all around her breasts. She squirmed and whimpered, sounds he planned to hear every day at least twice a day.

"Dark Horse?" she asked as he slid down between her legs, putting them over his shoulders.

"Not a word. All I want to hear are little loving whimpers." He spread her

"You need a condom. We don't know what they...he gave me." Her breath came out in a rush. "Please."

Dark Horse smiled. "Relax, little flower. I spoke with Red Hawk about this. It would seem when he healed you, the Great Mother herself intervened, making sure you are whole and ready for children."

"What?" Lilly squeaked and would have sat up if he hadn't grabbed her breasts, holding her in place.

"Well, it seems I'm going to have to tie your sweet body down." He started to get up but saw the fear in her gaze. "Lilly." He nipped the side of her thigh, squeezing her nipples and breasts. "I'm here, baby. Eyes on me."

When Dark Horse knew she was fully back with him, he buried his tongue inside her pussy, refusing to allow that dead asshole in on any of their loving.

She grabbed onto his braid as her hips rose, pushing his tongue deeper into her.

He slid two fingers into her pussy. Dark Horse sucked her clit into his mouth, rubbing her sensitive spot, watching his flower bloom under his touch. Her scream had him smiling as she flew apart.

But what he wasn't expecting was her father to come storming into the room with a gun pointed at them. He rose, shielding her with his body.

"She's fine, Darvin. I just didn't know your little girl was a screamer."

She squealed and gave him a smack upside his head.

"Her mother was, too." He turned to leave, encountering Running Wolf and Stephan both there with weapons and smiles.

"I'm never leaving this room again," Lilly whispered, yanking the blanket up over their bodies.

Her father closed the door, leaving Dark Horse alone with Lilly. "Did you just smack me on the head?" He rolled onto his side, sliding his hand back down her stomach to her pussy where he slapped it, bringing a dazed expression to her face.

"What are you doing to me?" she whispered, grabbing onto his arm.

"Oh, little flower I've just started, but I think we need to do something about the loudness of your vocals. Of course, I love to hear you scream, but we do have guests and a wee little one who needs her rest. Not to mention a teenager who does not need to hear screaming." He earned another glare and a shove at his chest.

He leaned over and bit down on her nipple, halting any further action from her. "I'm going to have to work with you to get over your fear of being tied down, but for now, will you stay where I put you?"

***

Lilly's emotions and hormones were all over the place. One look from Dark Horse and she was a pile of goo.

But...she glanced at the door, earning a slap to the side of her breast. "Eyes on me, little flower, nowhere else. I'll make sure you won't scream like you did before." Getting up off the bed, Dark Horse went to the dresser and pulled out a pair of socks. Stretching them, he returned to the bed.

"See how stretchy these are? You'll be able to remove them anytime you need to. But I want you to try and keep them on for me." He tied one of her arms, loosely.

"Tomorrow, we'll go shopping. I think some nice silk scarfs will work best for you, till you are used to bringing tied up. There are a few other things we need to get before we head to New Orleans anyway." He lifted her arms over her head and secured them to the headboard.

Lilly tugged at her hands, sucking in her breath in when she couldn't get loose.

Dark Horse sat on the bed, hovering over her, running his finger down her cheek. "Eyes on me, little flower. See that you are safe with me. If it's too much, we'll stop right here. We have time. I'm not going anywhere. There will be no other women for me." He placed a kiss on each of her cheeks then covered her mouth in a scorching kiss that had her toes curling and the heat once more rising through her body.

He lifted his head, waiting for her answer.

"Replace the demons, Dark Horse. Give me something to cling to when things get bad," Lilly whispered

Dark Horse lay down next to her and cupped her breast, running his finger over her nipple. "You have a body I could play with for hours, but you need sleep. Hell, we both need sleep." He sucked on the skin on her breast.

"I'm going to have hickies all over my body," she moaned.

"My body, and you'd better believe it. You'll carry my mark always." He sucked on her other breast, sliding his hand down to her pussy.

Her little nub already swollen and ready, a few rubs had her needing more as he carefully lifted up over her. His cock brushed her pussy lips a few times before he inched it into her.

Dark Horse lifted her legs and placed them on his shoulders, slowly sliding all the way into her. "You're so beautiful, my little flower." Lilly knew he meant every word.

This wasn't someone taking her against her will, this was a man who had risked his life for her. She strained to touch him, but her hands wouldn't move.

"I want to touch you," she moaned as he pulled out and thrust back in.

"Soon." He held still for a few seconds then swirled his hips. "Are you okay?"

No flashbacks so far. Lilly nodded. "More, please." She tried to move her hips, but Dark Horse held her still. "Don't," he ground out.

"Dark Horse," she whispered.

"That's right. Dark Horse. No one else. You are mine, and I don't share," he said, slowly lowering her legs and releasing her arms. He thrust in and out faster always hitting that one spot inside he had found earlier.

"Feel us together, little flower." He braced himself on his arms on either side of her head, as he covered her mouth kissing her, owning, claiming her.

Time didn't matter, and being quiet went out the window as she

156

gripped his shoulders, holding on to her lifeline. It was as if her body, sighed. Her muscles, the stiffness of her movements all seemed to work with this man who now owned her body

He surrounded her with his love, his protection, showing her with his loving that he wasn't going to go anywhere. He swirled his hips, hitting spots that she knew existed, but had never experienced.

All the defenses Lilly had put up around her, this man was slowly tearing them down and surrounding her with his own wall, showing her how love should be between a man and woman. Between him and her.

She broke the kiss, looking up at him. "What are you doing to me?" she whispered, as he nipped her bottom lip.

"Loving you, just loving you." He kissed her again, but this time he hit that spot, sending her body into warp drive. He took her scream, adding his own groans as their bodies took over, hers exploding in pleasure so intense Lilly swore Dark Horse had set off fireworks inside her head.

A few minutes later, Dark Horse lifted his head smiling, as he rolled over and pulled her up onto him, never pulling out of her. "You're mine, little flower. Sleep." He pulled the cover over them.

"Hmm, how are you going to sleep, with me crushing you?" She placed a kiss on his chest, running her fingers up and circling his neck. "Thank you, Dark Horse."

"You'll never squish me, and I have a feeling I'm going to sleep like a baby with you in my arms." He placed a kiss on the top of her head, squeezing her ass cheeks. "There will be no thanking me. I love you, Lilly. I know it's quick and strange, but you are my home. I could care less where we are as long as you are at my side and safe." He rubbed his chin on the top of her head. "Sleep, little flower. I have you."

For the first time in a while she was safe.

She sighed and closed her eyes, enjoying his touch on her back, realizing how tired she truly was.

Chapter Fifteen

One of the things I've been taught by Native American elders is the importance of patience, of waiting to do things when the time is right.

Joseph Bruchac

Dark Horse was alone in bed, and that pissed him off. Dark Horse swung his legs off the bed when the door cracked open.

"Well, poop. I wanted to surprise you," Lilly held up a tray of food. "I cooked breakfast."

He smiled, the ache in his chest gone as he scooted back against the headboard, covering his cock with the sheet. She was still a little nervous around him.

"I just woke up, but I have to say I was disappointed I didn't have my little flower next to me when I woke. This does make up for it. Come." He patted the spot next to him. "Let me see what you have."

"You were sleeping so soundly I didn't have the heart to wake you." She placed the tray on his lap before climbing over him. "Plus, you were so cute. You snore, but it's real light."

"I don't snore." He took a big bite of the omelet she made for him. "Oh, my god, what is this?" He stuffed more into his mouth.

She laughed. "You might want to slow down. It gets pretty hot."

"Lilly, is that your famous omelet I smell?" her father yelled through the door, knocking on the it before peeking in.

"Yes, Daddy, and I made five more for whoever gets to them

first..." she said, but her father was already gone.

His mouth started to warm up. "Good, but damn hot... You should put warnings on these," Dark Horse grabbed a handful of her hair and kissed her hard. "Morning, little flower. Thank you for the food, but please don't leave the bedroom till I'm up. It's important I know where you are at all times."

More pounding on their door had Dark Horse growling. "What?"

"Can we steal Lilly? There is about to be a fight here since there are not enough omelets to go around." Stephan peeked into the room.

"Please," Running Wolf asked. " Little Gypsy stole mine."

"Did not, you fibber. You gave it to Emma, so don't even go there," Kizzy yelled.

"Well, since you gave one to Emma, I guess I'll allow her to leave my side. We'll be out in a minute," Dark Horse set the tray aside. "Go get dressed before I change my mind." He moved to the dresser, grabbing clothes as she slid into the master bathroom.

"Want to share a shower?" She dropped the robe she wore.

Dark Horse slammed their bedroom door, shutting the others out.

He shut and locked the bathroom door, watching the water slide down her body as she lifted her face up to the spray.

"You going to stare at me all day, or are you going to help me with this ache I have?" She turned her heated gaze on him. He knew it took a lot for her to ask, and he wasn't about to deny his woman anything.

"And what kind of ache do you have? Is it one in your ass?" He stepped into the shower, closing the shower door behind him. He ran his hand over her round globe. "I don't think you are ready for me here, yet, but soon."

Lilly turned and wrapped her arms around his neck. "I haven't felt this... I don't know how to explain it. I know I shouldn't be dependent on you, but I am already. When I woke up in your arms, it was the most beautiful thing." Lilly cocked her head to the side. "I have to say good tears were involved.".

"Thank you, you've made me feel whole and needy it would seem."

She stroked his cock. "It's my turn."

Lilly dropped to her knees, water running down her head as she licked and then covered his cock with her mouth, sucking.

He put his hands on her head and guided her. "Suck harder, little flower." Dark Horse fucked her mouth slowly, careful not to gag her, but too quickly he was ready to release his seed.

He lifted Lilly and pushed her against the shower wall. "I want inside you before I release little flower," he told her quickly checking to make sure she was damp and ready for him.

"Hang on, baby. This is going to be hard and fast," Dark Horse warned, sliding inside her, moaning. "You feel so good." Dark Horse grabbed onto her ass cheeks as she wrapped her legs around him and dug her fingers into his shoulders.

"Faster, harder, please," she begged, resting her head against the shower wall.

"little flower," he growled, rotating his hips, hitting that special button he found last night, thrusting in and out of her faster and harder, watching his Lilly give him everything she had.

"Love me, Dark Horse," Lilly begged.

"Always," he growled, covering her mouth, claiming her again, showing her how much she meant to him. Their kiss was a dance of love.

"Dark Horse," she whispered into his mouth, breaking the kiss. Her pussy squeezed his cock as her orgasm rolled over her.

Quickly, he covered her mouth, knowing her loud vocals would embarrass her. Not being able to hold off any longer, Dark Horse release his seed, hoping the Great Mother would grant them a child, a little girl just like his Lilly. When her trembling slowed, he uncovered her mouth

"Wow, and thank you. I was loud again." She giggled, and he couldn't help but laugh.

"Come on. Let's get cleaned up. You have some hungry people out there waiting for food." Dark Horse lowered her to her feet and cleaned her from head to toe.

"Damn it, Dark Horse." She glared at him as he pushed her out of the shower. "Now, I'm all... Well, you know."

"Needy." He grabbed a towel and dried her off. "You'll have to wait for later, I'm afraid. Now, get going." He slapped her butt, pushing her toward the door.

"You might want to wear something warm. We had a freeze last night." Lilly went to the dresser and pulled out a pair of jeans and sweater. But when she reached into another drawer, pulling out one of the sexiest camisole and panties that he had seen.

Dark Horse walked over to take them out of her hands staring at them then her.

"I told you I had a thing for sexy undergarments." She shrugged. "That's one of my favorites, even though I can't wear a bra with this. It does have some support for these big things." Lilly cupped her breasts.

"Get dressed or I'm going to have you back on that bed, tied down and spread." Dark Horse shoved the clothes back into her.

Watching Lilly wiggle into her clothes, he gritted his teeth as he tried to stuff his hard cock into his pants and zip them.

She giggled and ran for the door.

"This isn't over, little flower." He carried the tray into the kitchen behind her.

"You going to finish that?" Soaring Eagle gestured at his plate.

"Yes, I'm going to finish my food. All of you are acting like you're damn starving." He sat down, but before he could take another bite, Lilly grabbed his plate.

"Let me heat this for you. There's fresh coffee coming, too." She slid his unfinished omelet into a pan then started cutting up more food. "How many more omelets do I need?"

"My nephew is ungrateful thing, not respecting his elders." Stephan glared at Kizzy's brother.

Mason snorted. "Get up earlier and maybe you could have gotten one."

"Not to worry. I'll have some more made in a few minutes." Lilly poured fresh coffee into a cup and traded it for Dark Horse's cold one.

"My daughter could have been one of those famous chiefs you see on TV, but nope, she followed in her momma's footsteps, becoming a nurse, wanting to help people," Darvin took a sip of coffee. "When she gets in a baking mood, I gain the pounds."

Lilly rolled her eyes. "Well, it looks like I'll have to cut back on the sweets and start making some more healthy things for you." She pointed her knife at her father.

"Now, you are just being downright mean. I think Dark Horse

needs to spank you. I want my molten lava cake."

"Molten lava cake." Kizzy shook her head. "Okay, you so need to make that before I leave."

Lilly flipped the eggs she was making before turning and staring at him. "How about I make a celebration dinner tonight? But I want to go shopping."

"No." Dark Horse took a sip of coffee then set down his mug before yanking her onto his lap. "Make a list. I'll have someone get you whatever you want, but today we are staying here at the house. I lost you yesterday, and I'm not sharing you with the outside world yet. It's bad enough I have to share with them," he grumbled, making Running Wolf laugh.

"Now you know how I felt the next day," Running Wolf, placed his hands on Kizzy's shoulders.

Kizzy snorted. "Like that stopped you from anything ..." She frowned and glanced at Emma. "Never mind."

"So, all that screaming last..." Emma's gaze jumped to him then to Lilly who groaned as she got off his lap and returned to the stove.

"Never mind what that was," Lilly mumbled, as everyone burst out laughing.

"Remember, I have your food here." Lilly stomped her foot, glaring at them all.

"Lilly Rose!" Her father growled.

"Your food is ready. Excuse me." Lilly turned off the stove and headed toward the back door, grabbing a jacket.

"Damn it," Dark Horse headed to get his boots and coat, but Emma stood in the hallway, eyes flooded with tears.

"I didn't mean to hurt her. I guess we all have issues." Emma sniffled.

Dark Horse pulled the teenager into his arms. "It is going to take all of us time to get to know each other. But Lilly needs us both and honey, I think this has just been waiting to come out and has nothing to do with what went on in the kitchen. Now, go finish your breakfast. We don't want her food to go to waste." He placed a kiss on the top of her head. "We'll work this out." Dark Horse said. "And don't allow anyone to eat my food."

She gave him a little smile. Emma needed them as well.

But, first, Dark Horse needed to find his upset woman.

Chapter Sixteen

Change is the end result of all true learning.
Leo Buscaglia

Lilly knew two of Dark Horse's men followed her, but right now she didn't give a damn, and she had no idea what the hell was wrong with her.

Hell, she could take a joke, but the tears still rolled down her cheeks as she hugged herself, staring at the creek that ran through the property they occupied.

She took a deep breath and wiped the tears away. All her life, Lilly had known what she wanted, but now nothing made sense. Especially, her feelings for a certain man. Lilly swore if it were the old days, Dark Horse would be riding a horse.

She sat on a stump, staring out at the water, smiling at the mental image of Dark Horse in tight buckskin pants.

She shook her head. "Damn, he'd be even hotter in those."

"That better be me you are talking about, little flower," Dark Horse growled, sitting down next to her, before lifting her into his lap. "Now what would I be hot in?"

She laughed and rested her head on his chest. "A pair of buckskin pants, like in the old days. I can so see you with war paint on, riding a horse, getting ready for a raid."

"I happen to have a few horses and own a few pairs buckskin pants. Although I've never been on an actual raid, unless you count what we've done for others over the last six years." He stared down at her. "How can I help?"

Lilly listened to the gurgling sounds of the water hitting the stones and banks.

"I was fine with the joking around, but as I finished making the food...I froze. With everything that has happened I don't know what to do. For so long I concentrated on living day by day. Before that I took care of Papa and worked. Everything is gone. They took so much. I feel lost."

"Would you allow me to help? I'm here for you, Lilly."

"How? You have so much going on, you shouldn't have to be worrying about me. If this is going to work between us, there has to be balance. You can't do everything. You're not Superman." Lilly glanced up at him, and he smiled.

"You don't know that. Maybe if I put on my buckskins, you'll think I'm Superman," he teased her, hearing two snorts from behind them.

Dark Horse growled. "There will be no comments from the peanut gallery, and I thought we were alone."

"You were, but Kizzy was worried about Lilly, and we got news about Raining Song's people." Running Wolf sat on the other stump, pulling Kizzy down into his lap.

"I still can't fathom why he would join with Fuzz and his group. It just does not make sense." Lilly shook her head.

"It would seem Raining Song and a few of his men were indebted to him for gambling and some other things. Black Bull informed me that since his wife died, Raining Song has drifted and couldn't get back on the right path. His people would like to come here and help with the preparations. It would seem you are to become Chief Dark Horse," Running Wolf teased him.

"What?" Dark Horse growled, and Lilly couldn't help but laugh.

"They want to join you here, set up tents and such, storing what they'll need for the tunnels but getting rid of everything else. They've already voted, and not one person objected. How many acres of land are here?"

"Wow?" Lilly looked up at Dark Horse.

"This was a working farm. We just took two and a half acres, but I know the rest is still there, over three hundred and forty, with twenty of it being forest so there is plenty of land. I'll have Stephan check into purchasing it. We are going to need to speak with the surrounding land owners, too. Lilly since you know pretty much everyone, I will let you find out what you can. Maybe they'd like to help. I'll also need a list of everyone who lived in town. We need to see if there are more of Fuzz's men roaming around and what people are doing since most of the town has been damaged."

Lilly smiled. "Thank you."

His nose touched hers as he leaned down. "I will have a list for you of things that need to be accomplished each day. If they aren't, we can discuss what the problem is." He grinned. "Kizzy isn't the only one who likes order."

Running Wolf nodded. "You know, I think you have the right idea. Maybe having a list will keep this Little Gypsy and out of trouble."

Both she and Kizzy snorted. "One thing about women is we can do many things at once, so bring on the list, baby, especially if it will help with all that you have going on." Kizzy said. "Don't think I don't hear you at night talking with my idiot family and your men headed to Canada."

"I think this is why the Great Mother paired us. We're perfect for each other." Running Wolf placed a kiss on Kizzy's cheek.

Lilly frowned, getting up and moving toward the creek. "Is it just me, or is the Earth opening up again?" Dark Horse came up behind her.

"No, I've been watching it. Running Wolf, what do you think?"

"I have a feeling the Great Mother is showing us something," Running Wolf joined them at the creek's edge.

"Maybe the tunnels we've been searching for?" Kizzy said. "If it is, it's going to be a few days before anyone can explore that with the area soaked from the creek."

Lilly glanced up at Dark Horse. "Since we have to wait a few days, why not have Raining Song's people over for a bonfire. We could see how many people we're talking about and I'd like to invite a few of my friends that I know who will help. Maybe before this trip to New Orleans we can assign some of them different things to accomplish while we are gone?"

Dark Horse wrapped his arms around her and yanked her body against his.

"Wonderful idea. Let's head back so we can start contacting these people and make plans. Get your pen and paper out, ladies. Your first list of the day is for today." Dark Horse nipped her nose then swatted her ass. "Let's go. I'll have Jay Bird put someone on this area to keep watch."

***

Dark Horse sat on the picnic table, watching as the men from Raining Song's reservation arrived. Over one hundred and twenty, from what Soaring Eagle had told him when they returned from their walk. All of them insistent that they come over right then and there, that it couldn't wait.

He shook his head and smiled, remembering what Soaring Eagle had told him and given him a few hours ago. His little flower had actually cried when the man had given him another Eagle feather, telling him he would make a great leader for his people.

"You getting over the old man's words yet?" Jay Bird sat next to him, watching as men arrived, talking with each other.

"No. How the hell could all of these men accept me for their leader? It's mind boggling as Emma would say. I mean really let's be realistic, what do they know of me?" Dark Horse released the breath he was holding.

Two men stepped forward, each carrying a box.

"My name is White Fox, and next to me is Tom Cat. I was the treasurer, and Tom Cat was in charge of the land, assigning homes and such." White Fox bowed his head.

"A week ago, our medicine man told us a story we didn't want to believe, but sadly it was true. Our chief had gone against everything that was taught us," Tom Cat informed him.

"But, three nights ago, each of us"—White Fox waved his hand to encompass the men behind them—"received the same vision about you." He smiled. "The Great Mother has chosen you as our next leader." White Fox held up the box for him. "For you."

The box was long, oddly shaped, and a little bit heavy. He took it from White Fox and opened it to find what appeared to be an ancient shield, made of metal.

"Each chief should have his own shield," White Fox told him as Dark Horse ran his hand over the engraving. *The Dark Horse Clan.*

"And each chief should have a headdress." Tom Cat laid the

other box on top of the shied, lifting the lid. "As your medicine man gave you the feather, ours gives you this. He's been working on it nonstop over the last week."

Words left him... On one side of the headdress, woven in beads, was a replica of his knife, the same one he was going to have tattooed on Lilly's back, while on the other side was Soaring Eagle's mark, showing him as Dark Horse's father.

Tears filled his eyes. Lilly and Kizzy emerged from the house, offering the men drinks, drawing their attention away from him. He glanced up at his flower, his sun.

"It would seem my son has lost his words. Who is your medicine man? I'd love to meet him and thank him." Soaring Eagle thumped Dark Horse's shoulder.

It would seem his family would always take care of him. The men moved aside as an elderly man, using a walking stick made his way toward them.

Dark Horse rose from the table as did Jay Bird, bowing their heads at the man who radiated power. A man much like his Soaring Eagle.

"You honor me and I thank you for gift," Dark Horse was beyond impressed as the man took headdress.

"I am called, Kaapo Lakely. If you notice, your flower is also part of your life circle. Your flower is the center of you, Dark Horse. Every man here knows..."

Dark Horse held out his hand, enfolding hers.

"As she is your sun, the two of you together are our hope. I see many grandchildren for your father, Soaring Eagle," Kaapo Lakely told them.

Soaring Eagle snorted. "I better have at least three by the time this is over and I see them again."

Lilly turned and was going to say something smart, but shook his head. "Not now little flower." He leaned down and kissed her lips. "Go help Emma. She's having a rough time. If you need me, yell." He pushed toward their soon to--be adopted daughter was right now surrounded by a few men, which had her stiff as a board.

"Relax. Lilly will help her. I'm sure she's just—" Soaring Eagle was saying as one of the men knocked Lilly on her ass, getting to close to Emma

Dark Horse pulled his knife out, heading for the man who dared to touch what was his.

"You have five seconds to tell me why I shouldn't slice him from ear to ear for touching my family, White Fox," Dark Horse growled

The offending asshole backed away and dropped to his knees, bowing.

Dark helped Lilly up.

"Dark Horse, please, it's not what it appears." Emma moved to step in front of the man, but Running Wolf grabbed her and pulled her to his side.

"I was dating his son before all of this stuff happened," Emma informed them.

"And that gives him the right to knock my woman down and threaten you?" Dark Horse demanded.

"No, it does not," the man on the ground said. "I know it's not an excuse, and I apologize to you and your woman, but our son is missing. Has been ever since he went to speak with Emma last week."

Dark Horse slid his arm around Lilly. "Have you seen his son, Emma?"

He shook her head. "I told him to stay away. It was getting bad, and I didn't want him hurt." Tears ran down her cheek. "But he wouldn't listen."

Kizzy approached, holding her daughter. "He's not dead, but I can't see where he is."

"He found our tunnels, or at least another way in. He's hurt, but if we can find him, I think he'll be okay." Lilly tapped her finger on his arm.

"Really? You think Chris Tom is still alive?" Emma smiled.

Lilly held out her hand. "Come. While the men discuss how to find him, we can make sandwiches and stuff for them."

Dark Horse nipped her ear. "The man should be gutted."

"The man was worried about his son as you would be if we had a son, right?"

Dark Horse put his knife away, to the sound of sighs. "Chicken shits." He swatted her butt and kissed the top of Emma's head, before turning to the man who still knelt before him.

"Get up. What is your name so I have it in case there is another incident?" Dark Horse punched the man in the nose as soon as he stood up. "Next time you have a problem with Emma, you come to me. She's my daughter, now."

The man nodded, rubbing his bleeding nose. "I apologize again for what I did."

Stephan tossed him a towel.

"I brought a map of the area and marked possible places to check. But I think we should have Kizzy and Lilly check it over. They might get a clue which area to search for the boy." Stephan spread the map on the table as Soaring Eagle came over, studying it with Kaapo Lakely.

174

"Do you know where we should start the search, Soaring Eagle?" Dark Horse asked. "What route do you think he would have taken, considering he would be trying to stay out of view."

"My name is Blue Carp, and if I know my son he'd stick to this route," the man he'd just punched informed him, pointing to a line on the map.

"Sorry, but he didn't go that way. He went some way that was...forbidden?" Lilly said, as she and Emma handed out sandwiches.

"My son wouldn't go into the old burial grounds," Blue Carp snapped.

Dark Horse spun, picked the man up by the collar, and shook him. "I've had enough of you. Get the hell out of my sight. That is the second time you have disrespected my woman. Next time, I won't hesitate to use my knife. Tom Cat take, him home while we search for his son. If you have any influence, I suggest a serious chat with him." Dark Horse threw the man away from the table. Tom Cat took Blue Carp's arm and led him away.

Kaapo Lakely frowned at the man's retreating back. "That man has never before gotten out of hand like this."

Soaring Eagle placed his hand on his shoulder. "Dark Horse?"

Dark Horse turned to the man he considered his father. "How can I lead these people if I want to kill one of their own? I won't be able to stop myself if there is a next time."

Lilly hugged him tight and said, "I think Emma can fill all of you in on Chris Tom's family. I have a feeling we are going to have him living with us also if what she says is true."

"What?" Kaapo Lakely glanced at Emma. "Speak, child. I would like to know why this is going on."

Emma moved in closer to him, and Dark Horse reached out, pulling her to his side. "There is nothing to be afraid of. What is going on, Emma?"

"The only reason why Chris Tom went home was to check on his mom. His father is a very violent man. I don't know how many times Daddy patched Chris Tom up because he didn't want to cause trouble."

"Emma, does he hit his wife?" Dark Horse asked.

"Chris Tom protected her. I haven't seen her lately, though, and I asked about her. That's what set him off tonight," Emma said.

Kaapo Lakely tapped his staff. "Dover, follow them back to his house, and make sure you check on his wife. If there are any signs of problems, take her to your home."

"It will be done. We had no idea." Dover left.

"He's a family member. I don't know how this can happen?" The old man sagged, suddenly seeming worn down.

Dark Horse nodded. "Even we have those who have given up or chosen the wrong path. But right now, we concentrate on the boy. Then I'll make sure to see what this man has done and if he can be helped." But inside Dark Horse just hoped the mother was still alive. The boy would need her.

For the next hour hours, over two hundred men and women searched for the boy, till his own Lilly called out with Kizzy right next to her.

They stood on a small hill over the ancient burial site, knowing it would upset the others if they were to set foot into the burial grounds.

Running Wolf approached. "What's up, Little Gypsy?"

"Over there by that oak. Lilly and I have been trying to figure out what the hell it was, but I swear that oak tree has moved over the past hour," Kizzy told them.

Lilly placed her hand over Dark Horse's. "Look to the left, on the ground. There used to be a grave there, not a hole."

"How the hell did we miss that?" Dark Horse placed a kiss on Lilly's cheek.

"Most likely the branches. It took us a good hour to figure out what was going on. I mean, we didn't even feel the ground moving from here," Kizzy grabbed a bottle of water out of the case on the ground.

"Stay here, you two. Let's hope we have found the next entrance to the tunnels. If it is, they are massive." Dark Horse trotted down the hill with Running Wolf. Soaring Eagle and Kaapo Lakely met them at the bottom.

The four of them circled the hole, staring down into it as a man brought over flashlights and rope.

"We'll go down. You are needed in case something happens," one of the men from Raining Song's clan volunteered, tying the rope around the tree and lowering himself down the hole, followed by three other men.

One of the men shouted up to them. "We have the boy! He's going to need medical help, though. He's not in good shape."

Dark Horse turned to the medicine man. "Lilly is a nurse."

Soaring Eagle and Kaapo Lakely both stared up on the hill. "They are both married to you and part of our world. The Great Mother brought her to you. Please have her come help."

Red Hawk came over with a board. "I'm here, too."

"You are too exhausted from healing Lilly yesterday." Dark Horse called, "We need you, Lilly."

Lilly carefully moved down the hill, with Kizzy's help.

They pulled the battered young man from the ground.

Lilly checked him out with Red Hawk.

"Broken arm and leg. Don't know if it was from the fall or not. He's been beaten up, bad," Red Hawk concluded.

Lilly wrapped the wounds of the unconscious boy. "He needs to go to the hospital, Dark Horse."

Red Hawk nodded. "I've healed what I can, but he's too bad for me to do what I need to. In the hospital, he can get the help he needs." Red Hawk stood, helping Lilly to her feet. Tears ran down her face.

"I still don't know how a parent can do that to a child." His little flower wiped a tear away and melted into his embrace "I'd like to take Emma there and make sure he gets set up. Have my friends watch out for him and get him started in counseling, because he's going to need it if we are going to break this Running Wolf sighed. "I'll take them to the hospital, along with Emma and leave you to explore the tunnels. We'll be back in a couple of hours for your report."

"Yes, sir," Dark Horse replied. "Lilly, you will listen to everything Running Wolf says, yes?"

She smiled. "Yes, sir," Lilly repeated.

"Woman." He yanked her into his arms. "Be safe, my, little flower." He covered her mouth in a hard, quick kiss, before releasing her to his best friend.

"Relax. I'll be fine. Plus, I want to talk with the doctors and nurses there about helping us." Lilly patted his arm and left.

Dark Horse watched them walk away then grabbed on to the rope and climbed down into the hole. What he saw left him speechless.

Chapter Seventeen

*Time seems to stand still as history comes to hit you in the face,
repeating the failures of mankind and giving them a chance to
redeem themselves, will they listen?*
Chief Dark Horse

Lilly took a deep breath taking in everything around the ER and realizing she didn't miss it at all. Oh, she loved the work she had done there and the people she worked with, but now her life had switched direction, Dark Horse.

"Is this where you worked?" Kizzy asked, one arm around Emma who stood between them.

"It is, but it's weird seeing it now. It's like I'm seeing it as a different person, if that makes sense?" Lilly shook her head.

"It makes perfect sense. You've gone through a life-changing event, you're different, and your life's goals and values have changed," Soaring Eagle came up with Running Wolf. "You have done the boy good, Lilly. Already, he is awake and speaking with your doctor friend, and a number of people have volunteered to help you and Dark Horse."

"You should be proud of yourself. In a few hours you have accomplished much," Soaring Eagle sounded so much like her father.

"I'm just glad Chris Tom is going to get the help he needs. I've seen traits continue on from one generation to the next. It needs to stop now, and I'm very happy my girlfriends are going to help us organize and that they actually believe me. I thought for sure they'd think I was nuts," Lilly snorted as they all moved toward the doors, heading back to the house.

"I'm afraid things are changing slowly around here already. Even the animals are reacting to the change. Most of the roads around here are starting to crumble. Already the Great Mother is taking things back." Soaring Eagle stepped outside. "It's going to storm tonight."

Lilly could smell the rain in the air. "We get some nasty storms. Maybe it's going to clean the Earth of all the blood that has been spilled. I always loved sitting out on the porch during a thunderstorm, watching the lighting."

Lilly got into the van, sitting next to Emma. "It's late, and I have to say I'm beat. How about some Chinese food for dinner?"

Emma and Kizzy nodded.

"I have to agree. Today has been one of those emotional roller-coaster type of days. Some good takeout and a glass of wine." Kizzy grinned. "Know a place you want to stop?"

Lilly smiled and nodded. "It's on the way back to the house. They are amazing people, too. There happens to be a wine store right next door, but do Running Wolf and the others drink?"

Soaring Eagle shrugged. "Some do. I like a beer once in a while and Dark Horse will drink nothing stronger."

Running Wolf peered in the rearview mirror. "Most of the men will drink a beer, but none of them will touch hard liquor. We've seen too many of our men turn into nasty drunks."

"I will have the occasional glass of wine to wind down at night or a shot of whiskey when circumstances call for it." Lilly pointed out the restaurant as they drove down the highway. "Thank God they were far enough from town, at least I hope so."

She was out of the door when Soaring Eagle grabbed her arm, stopping her.

"Easy there, Lilly. You always allow the warrior to go first, to make sure everything is okay."

"But I know the family." Lilly frowned.

"But when was the last time you spoke with them or have been here?" Running Wolf joined them with Kizzy and Emma as two of their men that had followed them on their bikes led the way inside. "From now on, Lilly, you have to take precautions, as Kizzy is supposed to."

Kizzy patted Running Wolf's chest. "Yes, I know, especially since the freaks seem to find me all the damn time."

"That's because you're special, Little Gypsy." Running Wolf bent down kissing the top of her head as one of the men nodded, holding the door open for them.

Inside, Lilly sighed at the damage that had been done, but the couple and their children were fine, trying to get back into business.

After exchanging hugs, and informing them where she was staying, she proceed to order the whole menu, doubled because of the number of people at the house.

With bags of food in hand, they returned to their vehicles. Emma rested her head on her shoulder. "Do you think we could go back to my place tomorrow? I'd like to go through my things."

Lilly gazed down at Emma. "Are you sure you're ready for this? We can just have everything put into storage until you're able." She squeezed her hand. "There is no time limit, Emma. We have plenty of help here."

"No, I need to do this. Plus, I'd like to get a few things of

Daddy's." Emma stared out the window.

"I'll speak with Dark Horse tonight. I see no reason why you can't. I'd like to hit a few stores tomorrow, so maybe we can do both things if Dark Horse isn't busy," Lilly reached over and squeezed her arm.

"Why don't we go in the early morning? We can have my uncle Stephan grab a U-Haul for the stuff she wants to keep. The garage has an extra shed that would store any of her possessions and then some. Plus, my uncles have been driving me crazy." Kizzy grumbled.

"Sounds good to me." Lilly nodded.

"We might want to wait to see what is going on at the house." Running Wolf smiled. "Dark Horse has been beeping my phone for the last hour, wondering where we have been. It would seem he's not liking being apart from Lilly too long." Running Wolf glanced at her in the mirror, smiling.

"We've been gone what four hours, jeez." But Lilly also couldn't wait to see the handsome warrior.

"Knock it off. If I'm not mistaken, you had a little fit when Kizzy and I went shopping one day?" Soaring Eagle gave Running Wolf a frown that had him groaning.

Kizzy laughed. "We had so much fun testing each other that night. Now, tell me I know you were seeing something at the ER, Lilly."

"You are good." Lilly laughed. "The ER was shut down, abandoned, almost scary, haunting." Lilly turned to face Kizzy. "Grass was coming up through the floor, and animals were inside. So many machines, medicine still in there and wasted. The only thing with my visions they could happen or not. Time frame I never know, and I hate it."

Kizzy frowned and peered up at Soaring Eagle. "Did you get anything?"

"Not a thing. I have a feeling Lilly's gifts pertain to future events. If I'm not mistaken, it's how the Irons found out about what is going to happen?"

Lilly nodded, a knot in her stomach as tears filled her eyes. "If I'd just kept my mouth shut."

"No, dear. If it wasn't for you, they would have found out somehow. I believe your warning saved a few people. Remember what your father accomplished in so little time. You couldn't help if that crooked sheriff took advantage of it. Are you hearing me, Lilly? Or do I need to have to speak with Dark Horse?" Soaring Eagle's voice dropped.

"Why would you tell Dark Horse I think I caused what happened? That makes no sense. He can't stop me from thinking that or believing it. No one can."

"Never and I mean never think they won't try and convince you otherwise." Kizzy leaned over and whispered, "It's better to agree with them."

"And don't think we won't be talking about that later, either," Running Wolf growled from the front, making Kizzy jump.

Lilly couldn't help but smile and Emma giggled as Kizzy sputtered, "You're a pain my ass, literally."

As soon as they pulled into the drive, Dark Horse came out of the house and headed toward the van, every inch of him a predator and deadly, but he was her Dark Warrior.

The van door opened, and he held his hand out to her. She heard something about being gone, but
Dark Horse pulled her into his arms. "I heard you started to go

outside by yourself," he growled, grabbing a handful of her hair, pulling her head back, and staring down at her.

"Never by yourself, Lilly. You and Emma will always be with someone, no matter what. Is that understood?" he ordered

"What? You have to be kidding. Even on dates?" Emma jumped out of the van, drawing Dark Horse's gaze.

"What dates? Do you really think any boy is going to come and ask me to go out with you?" Dark Horse smiled, and it wasn't a good one.

"Hey, knock it off. You don't need to scare her. Of course she'll have dates." Lilly hit his stomach and tried to get away, but his grip on her hair only tightened.

His gaze dropped down to hers. "Only if they have the nerve to ask me, and did you hit me?" He tossed her over his shoulder. "We'll be inside in a few. Emma, not to worry. We'll speak further about this." Dark Horse laid his hand on her ass hard, heading toward the garage.

"You might want to know your Lilly believes she is responsible for what happened to the town," Running Wolf yelled as Dark Horse stepped into the garage, shutting the door hard as another swat came down on her ass.

"What the hell are you doing?" Lilly hit his butt. "Quit smacking my butt. And to think I missed your big lug head. What the hell was I thinking?"

Dark Horse lowered her onto the hood of a car. "That is twice you have hit me, little flower," he growled, grabbing the bottom of her shirt and lifting it over her head before she knew what he was doing.

"What are you doing? Anyone could walk in here?" Lilly tried to grab her shirt back, but he threw it onto the roof of the car.

"I'm going to show you how much I missed you and explain why what happened to your town wasn't your fault." He unsnapped her jeans and yanked them off her. "And if you are really good, I won't spank you for hitting me."

Dark Horse stared down at his little flower. By three hours after she left, he'd been unable to concentrate, worried... He had ordered everyone out of the tunnels, telling at them, telling them to return tomorrow when they could see better and had the equipment to explore further.

He ran his hands up her stomach to her breasts and squeezed. "Never in all my life have I felt as empty as when you left. I know it was only for a few hours, but it was too long, my Lilly." He met her gaze. "I have a feeling this connection is only going to get stronger. I'm going to have to tie you to my side."

"Dark Horse," she whispered. "I felt the same way. All I could think about was you. It was like part of me was missing."

He studied her for a moment. "What's wrong, little flower?"

"I had one of my visions today in the ER." She lifted her gaze to his. "I'm scared, Dark Horse, really scared. The place had animals running around it, grass growing through the floor, vines growing up the walls. How can we do this?"

"We have no choice. It's our destiny, but I promise I'll be right beside you and any time you need me I'll be there." He pushed her back onto the car, and she screeched, glaring at him.

"It's cold damn it," Lilly grumbled, and he laughed, covering her mouth with his, tasting a little honey. "I need to be in you, little flower," he whispered against her lips, sliding his hand down between her legs and finding her damp and ready for him.

"I think someone protests to much about being spanked. We will explore that later. Stay." He unfastened his pants, his cock hard and ready as he set it free from its confinement. "Wrap your legs around me, baby." Dark Horse slid into her warm body. "God you feel amazing." He lifted her up, wrapping his arms around her and pulled slowly out to thrust back in. But first, he needed to correct something. Dark Horse stopped all movement, staring down at Lilly. "Now, you want to tell me why you feel so guilty?"

She tried to get him to move, but he held her still, even though it was pure torture for him.

"This is so not fair and not the time to talk about it." She nipped his shoulder, and he smiled.

"Oh, it's the perfect time, and I can do that, too." He bit down on her shoulder.

"Dark Horse!" she cried, out as he pulled out and thrust back into her. But she wasn't the only one affected by what he did.

Lilly's pussy tightened; her nails dug into his shoulders. "Oh my god. What are you doing to me," she whimpered as a small orgasm ran through her. But it wasn't enough.

Growling, Dark Horse started to move harder and faster into her, covering her mouth as she stiffened and her eyes got big. "Come, little flower. Give me all that you have," he growled, his own orgasm upon him. His seed shot into her, filling her as he ran his tongue over the spot he had bitten, kissing it as he tried to catch his breath.

He turned around, resting his ass against the car, staring at the beauty in his arms. "Lilly, remind me to show you the scar where this Fuzz got me six years ago. You didn't do this, Lilly. He knew something was up long ago, and has been trying to stop us on our journey. If anything, maybe I caused this. He was so angry the last time we met, that he didn't kill me." Dark Horse shrugged. "We'll never know. But we need to move on now. We have a hard road ahead of us. There is no room for guilt." He placed a kiss on her neck. "How come I smell food on you?"

Lilly giggled. "Because we got Chinese, a bottle of wine for Kizzy and me, and some beer for you guys. I want to sit on the front porch and watch the storm come in." Lilly rubbed her cheek on his shoulder just as the rumble of thunder could be heard in the distance.

"Well then, let's get dressed and eat so we can watch this storm come in. We have a lot to discuss too. I have some news about the tunnels you might find interesting."

Dark Horse helped Lilly get dressed, but she kept frowning and turning to look toward the darkening skies out the window. "What's wrong?"

"I don't know, but something or someone is coming, and I have a bad feeling." She rubbed her hands up and down her arms.

He scooped her up and made a dash for the house where, he found Running Wolf holding Kizzy in his arms on the swing. "Her, too?"

Soaring Eagle stepped outside. "It would seem this Fuzz wasn't the real threat, because whatever is coming this way is worse. The Great Mother is going to test us all once more."

His words filled Dark Horse's heart with dread as he sat down, holding tight to the most precious thing in his life. "How do we prepare?" He ran his hand up her back. He had a feeling this would be their final test as a group, as a family, before they all split in separate directions.

No one spoke for a long time, everyone staring at the approaching storm as Lilly curled up closer to him. "We'll make it, all of us, but others will not." Lilly's voice cracked when she turned to stare at him then at Kizzy who had tears running down her cheeks, nodding.

"Death is not the end. The end is when your soul finally rests," Soaring Eagle whispered. "The next battle will be not of man, now, but of the past."

Sign up for the Decadent Publishing Newsletter here

http://eepurl.com/SQ75f